Daring in the Desert

For Rowan Iona Howat
my granddaughter

Daring in the Desert

Lilias Trotter

Irene Howat

CF4·K

10 9 8 7 6 5 4 3 2 1

Copyright 2016 Irene Howat

Paperback ISBN: 978-1-78191-777-0

epub ISBN: 978-1-78191-877-7

mobi ISBN: 978-1-78191-878-4

Published by
Christian Focus Publications,
Geanies House, Fearn, Tain, Ross-shire,
IV20 1TW, Scotland, U.K.
www.christianfocus.com
email: info@christianfocus.com

Cover design by Daniel van Straaten
Cover illustration by Jeff Anderson
Map illustrated by Fred Apps

Contents

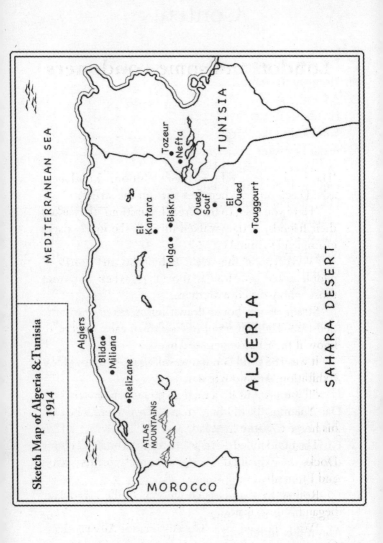

Sketch Map of Algeria &Tunisia
1914

MEDITERRANEAN SEA

TUNISIA

Tozeur
Nefta

El
Kantara   Biskra   Oued   El
                     Souf   Oued
Tolga   Touggourt

Algiers
Blida
Miliana
Relizane

ALGERIA

ATLAS MOUNTAINS

MOROCCO

SAHARA DESERT

London and some Londoners

'Have you been to the Great Exhibition?' Londoners asked each other, when they met on the street.

'Have you been to the Great Exhibition?' they asked their friends, as they walked through the lovely parks of England's capital city.

'Were you at the Great Exhibition on Saturday?' people asked on Monday mornings, when they met those who worked with them.

Strangers on horse-drawn buses asked the same question. The drivers of horse-drawn cabs wanted to know if their passengers had been.

It was 1851 and London was all abuzz with the Great Exhibition. And no wonder.

'Tell me about it,' a man asked his cab driver.

'You must be kidding!' teased the driver, as he told his horse to move forward.

The man smiled. 'I've just come off a boat at Tilbury Docks,' he explained. 'I've been overseas for five years and I'm really out of touch.'

Rolling his eyes at such ignorance, the cab driver began his description.

'Well,' he said, 'it's like this. Prince Albert, that's Queen Victoria's husband, had a great idea. His idea was to have an exhibition that would show all the wonders

7

of the British Empire in one place. And, as the British Empire is full of wonders, he had to build a huge palace to hold them all.'

'A palace?' the man looked puzzled. 'Do you mean a palace like Buckingham Palace, where Queen Victoria lives?'

The driver roared with laughter.

'No,' he told his fare. 'Buckingham Palace is built of stone but the Crystal Palace is built of cast iron and plate glass. That's why it's called the Crystal Palace. And if you want to see it for yourself, you'll have to go to Hyde Park.'

'Isn't all that glass dangerous?' worried the man.

'You would think so,' the cab driver agreed. 'But I suppose Prince Albert had the best brains in the Empire working for him. I've no doubt that it's safe.'

As they clip-clopped along the streets, the cab driver rattled off facts and figures that he'd stored in his mind for just such a customer as the one he was carrying to Bishopsgate.

'The Crystal Palace is 564 metres (1,851 feet) long and 39 metres (128 feet) high. It's made of 294,000 huge panes of glass attached to a cast iron skeleton. Some people thought that it would never stand up. But even when the great choir sang the Hallelujah Chorus at the opening of the Exhibition it stood as firm as if it was made of bricks and mortar. Mind you,' said the driver, 'I let it settle before I went to see it. I didn't want it to crash down on my head.'

The man in the cab was fascinated and wanted to know more. 'What's being exhibited in the Crystal Palace?' he asked.

'What's not!' laughed the cab driver. 'There are treasures from every corner of the Empire,' he said. 'They've even got the Koh-i-Noor, the world's biggest diamond!'

'You're kidding!'

'No, I'm not,' the driver insisted. 'There are weaving looms and kitchen equipment, huge displays showing how steel is made and jewels by the dozen. Stuff that's been dug up from history is on show, and inventions that belong far in the future too. There are over 100,000 things to see, I'm told. And I believe it. If you go, you'll see big things and little things, new things and ancient things. And wait till I tell you what ….'

There was a long silence as the driver held his fare in suspense.

'There are public closets where you can …' the cabman coughed rather than finish the sentence.

What he was trying to say was that there were public toilets in the Great Exhibition in London in 1851!

For six months people flocked to the Crystal Palace. At first only rich people could afford to go because entry cost £3 for men and £2 for women. That was a great deal of money in the middle of the 19th Century. But after a while it was reduced to one shilling (5p) each and that brought people in their thousands and then their millions.

Altogether six million people visited, and that was more than the population of the U.K. at that time. Of course, many people went more than once. And here's an interesting statistic – 827,280 people used the public toilets, and they had to pay a penny to do so! That's where the expression 'spend a penny' comes from.

When the Great Exhibition closed, the Crystal Palace was taken to pieces and much of it was carted through London to Sydenham Hill. A splendid but smaller exhibition centre was built there that was meant to last for many years rather than just six months. Building work began in 1852 and Sydenham Hill fairly swarmed with workmen for the next two years.

London was THE place to be in the early 1850s. The Great Exhibition had brought it to the notice of the whole wide world. Queen Victoria was young and lovely. Prince Albert was full of ideas for the city and the country. People were optimistic about the future and felt that it was good to be alive, and to be in London.

On 14th July, 1853 one London family was much more interested in what was happening inside their home than out in the city. They were the Trotters of Devonshire Place House, not far from another of London's famous green spaces, Regent's Park. For that day, in that very beautiful house, a baby girl was born. She was named Isabella Lilias Trotter and right from the beginning she was known as Lilias, or Lily.

'She's tiny,' whispered Emily, who was Lilias's sister, and the next oldest to her in age.

'She's cute,' Jaqueline giggled. She was the next one up.

Then Lilias's brothers came to see the new baby.

'She a girl,' announced ten-year-old Edward and twelve-year-old Henry.

The two oldest boys in the family, William and Coutts, were teenagers and they just smiled at the new addition to their family and went back to what they were doing.

The Trotters were a very happy family, but it had not always been like that. Lilias's father had been married before and all the older children were born to his first wife. When she died the family went through a time of great sadness.

Two years later, Mr Trotter told William and Coutts, Edward and Henry that he was going to marry again and the boys wondered what kind of stepmother they would have. Their two little sisters were really too young to be worried. They needn't have been concerned for their father's new wife was a good and kind, loving and caring young woman – even if she didn't seem young to them! Lilias was her first baby and it was as though tiny Isabella Lilias Trotter cemented the family together.

'May we walk with the baby?' Jaqueline and Emily asked their nursemaid, when it came time for their afternoon outing, a month or two after Lilias was born.

'We'll have to ask Nanny,' they were told.

Nanny appeared in her uniform, the baby in her arms.

'The girls would like us to join your walk,' the nursemaid told her. 'May we do that?'

Nanny, who looked very serious but was good fun too, said that would be alright and they'd better go and get ready.

Getting ready to go out took a long time in the 1850s. The best dressed girls, and Jaqueline and Emily were among them, wouldn't go out the door without their hair brushed and their hats on, their dresses straightened and their boot buckles polished. And the baby? Lilias was tightly swaddled in a shawl and wrapped in a blanket even though it was warm outside. Her pram was high and more like the body of a small convertible car than a modern-day pram! Had a sailor seen them coming along the road, he might have thought that Nanny, Nursemaid, Jaqueline and Emily along with Lilias in her wonderful pram looked like stately galleons going out to sea!

The Trotters lived in a beautiful, and very expensive, area of London. Their part of the city was called Marylebone, which started life as a little village hundreds of years before. By the time Lilias was born the streets were lined with stylish Georgian houses, each with its own garden.

The houses were often built around squares with lovely gardens in the middle. It was a good place for children to live as Jaqueline and Emily discovered when they moved out of the care of nursemaids and into the kind and firm hands of their first governess.

Of course, having a governess meant spending most mornings in the schoolroom (yes, they had their own schoolroom!), but it also meant going to play in Regent's Park in the afternoons. The girls met their friends there and were able to run about freely – or as freely as their long frilly bloomers would allow!

As soon as Lilias was old enough, she and her sisters loved watching their father going off to work each day. And no wonder they liked watching for he went to work in a stagecoach. So there were horses to see and a friendly coachmen who always looked up and waved to them.

* * *

'Why can't we go to school like our brothers?' Lilias asked her governess, in the middle of a reading lesson one day. She was six years old.

William and Coutts, Edward and Henry all went to Harrow, one of the most famous schools in England.

'Young ladies don't go to school,' the governess said firmly.

'But I'd like to learn the kind of things that William and Coutts learn,' Lilias announced. 'I'd like to learn about science and mathematics and things like that.'

Her governess smiled. 'And I wonder what good learning science would do you. Young ladies have their own skills to learn, things that will help them to fit into society when they grow up.'

Lilias was suddenly interested, expecting these skills to be exciting.

'Well,' her governess said. 'As you'll meet many grand people from overseas when you're older, you have to learn some foreign languages. You need to be able to entertain guests, some of them very well-known and clever, and for that you need to learn about art and literature, about the theatre and music.'

'I like art,' Lilias agreed. But she wasn't convinced that learning to entertain even well-known and clever guests was ever going to be as exciting as science.

Lilias did like art and she was very good at both drawing and painting.

'Is that a starling?' asked Mrs Trotter one day, when she went into the schoolroom. She picked up Lilias's drawing pad and took it to the window to see it more clearly.

It was a sketch of a starling sitting just outside the window, and it looked so real that it might have flown away.

'That's beautiful,' Mrs Trotter said. 'His feathers are so well drawn.'

'Would you like to see some paintings, Mama?'

'I certainly would!'

Mrs Trotter sat down beside her daughter. The other children had gone out to play for a while but Lilias chose to stay in to finish her drawing.

'These are flowers from the garden,' the girl explained. 'I drew them one day and then painted them afterwards. I tried painting them in the schoolroom but it was better when I took my paints outside to the garden.'

'You could have picked the flowers and brought them in to paint,' her mother suggested.

Lilias thought for a minute.

'I didn't want to do that, Mama, for the poor flowers would just wilt and die.'

Mrs Trotter took the sheets of paper. She looked at the top one and then, very slowly, she looked at the rest.

'These are lovely,' she said quietly. 'I can almost smell the scent of the roses.'

Very slowly she and Lilias looked through the paintings. They were amazing considering they'd been done by such a young child.

That evening, after the children were sound asleep, their parents sat and talked.

'Lilias has a real gift for drawing and painting,' Mrs Trotter told her husband, who was himself a keen artist.

Together they looked through Lilias's paintings and finished with the drawing of the starling. Both agreed that their young daughter was a born artist.

Home and Away

You'll have worked out by now that the Trotter family was rich. And you'd be quite right. Alexander, Lilias's father, was in banking and work sometimes took him abroad. There were maids, nursemaids and governesses working for the family, and living with them. That meant that, when Lilias was five years old, her mother was able to go on a business trip to America with her husband, even though by then there was another child, a little boy called Alec.

'I'm going to miss you, Mama,' Lilias said, not long before they were due to leave.

'I'll miss you too,' her mother agreed, 'but I'll write to you telling you all about America.'

'What are you looking forward to most?' Lilias asked her father.

Mr Trotter didn't need any time to think about that.

'I'm really looking forward to going on the American railroads,' he announced, grinning like a boy setting off on an adventure, which was exactly what it felt like to him!

Mr and Mrs Trotter, their eldest son, William, and a maid were away for four months altogether. During that time their mother wrote to all the children. Lilias, especially, loved her letters and looked forward to the postman's arrival.

To us, today, the letters sent to a small child seem very grown up. For example, when telling Lilias about an American sunset, Mrs Trotter wrote that there was, '... the most exquisite shades of colouring from clear blue, shading to pale green, and then to a most glorious golden colour ...'

But young though she was, the little girl saw in her mind's eye the colours her mother described and she could paint them in her sketch pad too.

'What are you doing today?' Emily asked.

It was pouring rain outside and there was to be no afternoon walk with their governess.

'I'm going to paint the sunset Mama wrote about,' she told her sister.

And she did.

First she wet the paper all over so that the colours would have no hard edges when they dried. Putting some blue paint on her brush she dragged it across the wet paper and watched as it left a line ... but a line that moved. As she watched, the blue pigment moved along the wet sheet, fading as it went further from the line. Then she did the same with a deep golden yellow paint, taking it across the paper from the other side.

'What ARE you doing?' Emily demanded, grinning at her sister's antics.

'I'm making the paint move,' said Lilias, holding the wet sheet in the air, first with the top of the sheet upwards, then with one side of the sheet to the top.

Emily came over to watch and laughed. 'I don't know how you do it,' she said. 'That really does look like sky.'

Jaqueline joined them. 'Where did that green come from?' she wanted to know, for the painting showed a blue sky turning to green and then gold. But there was no green paint on Lilias's paint dish, only blue and yellow.

Lilias grinned. 'It's my secret, but I'll tell you. I put blue and yellow on the wet paper and, when the colours moved about on the sheet, they mixed together and made green.'

The governess was watching and listening. 'She's a clever little girl, that one,' she thought. 'Maybe one day she'll be a famous artist. I wouldn't be surprised.'

The Trotter home was not only full of children, there were pets too. One, a kitten, was Lilias's favourite. Now, if you've ever lived with a cat, even a young kitten, you'll know that they don't need defending; they can stand up for themselves.

This particular kitten, which was being teased by Lilias's oldest brother, scratched him for being annoying. Lilias, who didn't like to see the kitten teased, sprang at her brother, hit him with one hand and grabbed the kitten with the other.

Because she wasn't usually a violent little girl the family remembered that day for years. And she wasn't allowed to forget it either for that's the day her brothers nicknamed her Tiger Lily and the nickname stuck!

By the beginning of April each year the Trotters would start thinking about holidays.

'I wonder what we'll be doing this year,' was usually said by one of the sisters for the first time about then.

'I hope we go back to Cromer,' Emily said. 'I love it there.'

All that afternoon, as they walked in Regent's Park, the three girls talked about Cromer. They had been there several times and had good memories to discuss.

'I like sitting on the sand reading a book best of all,' said Emily.

Lilias said that her favourite things were hunting for wild flowers and then painting them.

'My favourite thing about Cromer,' said Jaqueline, 'is that it's in England!'

All three giggled and Jaqueline went on. 'I quite like studying French and German at home, but it's different having to speak it to French and German people!'

'I don't mind speaking it to them,' said Emily. 'But it's when they speak to me I have problems. Sometimes they speak sooooooo quickly!'

Lilias, the youngest of the three, knew exactly what they meant. But it didn't bother her one bit. She loved going to Cromer, on the north coast of Norfolk, and she loved family holidays in Europe just as much. There were always different and interesting things to see and different and interesting things to draw and paint.

Mr Trotter always took his paints on holiday with him and all the girls did too. Drawing and painting were very popular hobbies in the mid-19th Century, especially among girls from wealthy families. Visiting art galleries was another favourite thing to do, and Lilias and her sisters loved it.

In Mr Trotter's dressing room was a table that was special to all his children. There were drawers under the table top and each child in the family had his or her own drawer.

'These are your little gardens,' he told his children, one by one, as they grew old enough to enjoy the treat. 'And if I find anything that will be especially interesting to any of you, I'll put it in your little garden for you to find. Of course, if your brothers and sisters are also interested in what's in your garden, I'd like you to show it to them.'

Now, this sounds like a game for small children, but it was much more than that. When they were little, Mr Trotter put things in that little children love – pine cones, new coins minted that year and still shining, picture books and other such treasures. But as they grew older, they found more grown-up things in their garden drawers. Lilias was especially pleased when she found leaflets about art exhibitions, or science talks, or special news about the botanic gardens.

The two last drawers were for Alec and Margaret, Lilias's little brother and sister. Sometimes Mr Trotter wrote letters to his children and put them in their drawers to be found. He sounds like a kind and a thoughtful father.

In 1863, when Lilias was ten, she had a photographic portrait taken. She wore her best dress. It had long sleeves and a wide skirt, with a frill round the bottom that came well below her knees. The dress looks white in the photo but it may have been light coloured. Puffed sleeves were very fashionable and she was right up to date. In the photo Lilias's long dark hair has a centre parting and is tied in a bow at the back. She's holding a doll on her knee.

Photographs were serious things in those days. Ten-year-old Lilias looks serious in her photo but not at all moody. If you have seen photos taken in the 19th

Century, you'll see that people very rarely smiled, and very rarely showed their teeth. One reason for that was that when someone had toothache their tooth was just pulled out to stop the pain. So many folk kept their mouths shut to hide the fact that they were missing their front teeth! That certainly wasn't the case with Lilias!

Just a year after that photo was taken Mr Trotter started to feel unwell and it was as if a shadow fell over that usually happy home. There was no cure for his illness and he died when Lilias was only twelve and Alec and Margaret were quite small. It was still a very busy house, as all but her two oldest brothers were living at home, but it was a sad place. And for Lilias it was as if there was an empty space in her heart where her papa used to be.

A New Home

The only thing that comforted Lilias was the fact that her papa had gone to be with Jesus in heaven. She could never remember a time when she hadn't heard about Jesus from her mama and papa. They were Christians and they brought up all of their children to believe. But that still left the teenager with questions.

'Why did God allow Papa to die?' she asked her mother. 'Why didn't he make him better when he was ill?'

Perhaps you have asked these same questions when someone you love died. And the only answer, and probably the one that Mrs Trotter told her broken-hearted daughter, is that God always does what is right, even if it seems wrong to us.

'Papa's death has changed Lilias,' Jaqueline told her mother. 'She's always been nice – though she does have her Tiger-Lily days! But she's somehow more soft and gentle now.'

Mrs Trotter smiled. 'Yes, I've noticed that too. It's as if she's trying to shine a light in our home to make up for your papa not being here.'

Both Jaqueline and her mama suspected that Lilias had become a Christian. It probably was about the time that she lost her earthly father that the teenager came to know her Heavenly Father as her best of all friends.

One evening Jaqueline, Emily and Lilias were sitting on a window-seat talking. The two younger children were sound asleep in their beds.

'Everything's different now,' Emily said.

Lilias was puzzled. 'What kind of everything?' she asked.

Her sister smiled. 'Well,' she said, 'Coutts is at university in Germany.'

'And I wish that I was with him,' said Lilias. 'I'd love to be studying science. It's soooooo interesting.'

Emily ignored her and went on, 'William's working in the City and a grown-up man. Henry's in India with the Royal Engineers and even Edward's away from home.'

Jaqueline thought this was a little dramatic. 'Edward's only at King's College,' she reminded her sister. 'He's not that far away!'

'But he's going to Oxford next year,' Emily pointed out.

It was quite true. Things had changed.

There was another big change about to take place and the time had come for them to hear about it.

'Girls,' said Mrs Trotter, later that evening, 'there is something I have to tell you.'

Since their father died, Jaqueline, Emily and Lilias had grown up a great deal, and they realised from their mother's tone of voice that this was to be a serious talk. All three sat still and waited.

'I know you love this house,' began their mother. 'And I love it too. All my memories of your dear papa are here. However, now that the boys are up and away it is far too big for us. We are going to have to move.'

'But where will we go?' all three asked together. 'We've always lived in London.'

Mrs Trotter smiled. 'We're not going to leave London,' she said. 'In fact, there's a house just six blocks away in Montagu Square that I think would suit us nicely.'

'Tell us about it,' said Lilias, and she sat back to listen. The teenager had an artist's imagination and an artist's eye. If she heard something being described well, she could picture it in her mind.

'It's number 40 Montagu Square and it's part of a four-storey terrace. The building is made of brown brick, though the ground floor is faced with white stone. There is a wide front door with steps leading up to it. Above the door there's a very pretty fanlight.'

'I like fanlight windows above doors,' said Jaqueline. 'They make the inside so bright and cheery.'

'It certainly is very bright and cheery inside,' her mother told them. 'From the hall you can look right up through all four floors to a lovely window in the roof.'

'That's called a cupola,' Emily told her sisters.

Mrs Trotter agreed. 'I think all the houses in Montagu Square have cupolas.'

'Do they all look the same from the outside?' asked Jaqueline.

'Almost,' Mrs Trotter told her, 'but not quite. Number 40 has white stone round the windows and the others don't.'

Before very long the Trotter family had moved to their new home. Life had indeed all changed. It was an exciting time for the girls especially, but it was also a sad time for they all missed their father very much indeed.

Lilias's older sisters had finished with school work, but she and her younger sister and brother still had lessons at home each day.

'I wish I could do your lessons,' young Alec said. 'German sounds interesting. English is just boring.'

Laughing, Lilias explained that he had to learn English before he could learn German.

'Then I'll do French instead,' the boy announced.

His sister smiled. 'I'm afraid it's the same with French. If you don't know English grammar, you'll not learn to speak French well either.'

The Trotter girls never went to school, though their brothers did when they were older. To start with they had governesses who taught them all the usual kind of lessons. Then they had language teachers from both Germany and France. Of course, that meant that they learned to speak German and French very well indeed. Because Lilias had a good voice she also enjoyed singing lessons. But, although she was a really fine artist, she only had one short course in drawing. All the rest she learned from going to exhibitions in London and visiting famous galleries abroad.

Holidays - Trotter Style

Try to imagine the Trotter family going on holiday to Italy. They travelled by a stagecoach drawn by four horses. Of course, the same four horses couldn't take them all the way from London to Italy. Teams of horses were kept at post houses set out along the road. Most post houses kept six teams of horses. When the family arrived at a post house they stopped for a while, maybe had a meal, and then set off again with a fresh team of four horses. A full day of travelling would begin about 9 am and end forty to fifty miles later at 3 pm. Occasionally they set off at 7 am and travelled twenty miles before breakfast, but not often.

Lilias was always on the lookout for interesting things and her sisters were used to her squeals of delight. 'Look at the rows of vines!' she would say, taking out her drawing pad to do a quick sketch as they trundled by.

When people come back from holiday today they show their friends all their photos on their phones. Lilias would have shown her friends sketches of the places she'd been to and the things she'd seen. We know she kept holiday sketch pads because some of them still exist today.

Because Lilias Trotter came from a wealthy family she didn't have to work and, of course, that gave her time to do all sorts of other things. Having spent childhood holidays in Cromer in Norfolk, one summer, when Lilias was in her late 20s, she went back and helped with a summer mission there. Back home in London the young woman became a member of a Christian choir which sang at mission meetings in the city. Although she didn't have a job, Lilias worked hard at a whole number of things, all of them to do with telling others about the Lord Jesus Christ. One special interest was the Welbeck Street Institute.

'Tell me about it,' she was asked one day by her friend Louisa, who was visiting her home.

'It was started by Lady Kinnaird,' began Lilias. 'She wanted to help girls who had come to London to work. They needed somewhere to stay that wouldn't use up all the money they earned. For a small charge girls get a comfortable place to live and they're not alone. The Welbeck girls are a bit like a club. New girls come along feeling that they know nobody and before long they are friends with nearly everyone.'

'So it's a hostel,' Louisa said.

Lilias thought for a minute. 'Well,' she said, 'I suppose you could call it a hostel. But it feels much more like a big home from home. All sorts of things are organised for the girls. There are French and German lessons, choirs, sewing groups and, most important of all, there are Bible classes for them to come to, and most of them do.'

Louisa wanted to know where the girls worked.

'Some serve in shops,' her friend replied. 'Others are dressmakers and many are servants.'

'I'm sure they like what you do for them,' said Louisa. 'It sounds very worthwhile.'

Some years later Lilias was once again in Europe.

'October 1876,' wrote Lilias, at the top of a letter to a friend back home in England. 'I am writing this from a hotel near the St Gotthard Pass on our way from Switzerland to Italy. The views of the Alps are amazing.'

She drew a quick sketch of the pass on the sheet of paper, before starting writing again.

'I bought a sketchbook at Lucerne and I'm going to do sketches in it as we travel to Venice. Looking back at them will remind me of the wonderful countryside we've gone through. The climb up to the St Gotthard Pass was amazing, but the horses must have been so tired! And, as I'm tired too, I'll stop now and get back to writing to you tomorrow.'

That sketchbook, which can still be seen today, is full of pencil drawings and watercolour sketches of villages, mountain chalets, forests, Swiss cows and people in traditional clothes.

After they crossed the border into Italy, Lilias continued her artwork, capturing the beautiful lakes at Maggiore and Como in watercolours.

'I can hardly wait to see Venice again,' said Mrs Trotter. 'It's such a wonderful city.'

Lilias was also very excited. As their stagecoach reached the city she felt like a teenager rather than a young woman of twenty-three. Before long she was to feel very embarrassed rather than very excited.

Soon after arriving at their hotel, Mrs Trotter discovered that one of the most famous men in England was staying there too. His name was John Ruskin. He was an artist, an art critic and a writer.

'I would like to show some of your paintings to Mr Ruskin,' Mrs Trotter told Lilias. 'I think you are a very good artist and I'd like to hear his opinion.'

'But Mother, you can't do that!' gasped her daughter. 'I just like drawing and painting. I'm not a real artist!'

Mrs Trotter had made up her mind. Taking her pen, she sat down at the desk in her sitting room, picked up a sheet of paper with the heading, 'Grand Hotel, Venice,' and wrote the date.

Completely ignoring Lilias's arguments, she wrote, in the style of the day, 'Mrs Alex Trotter has the pleasure of sending Professor Ruskin her daughter's water-colours. Mrs Trotter is quite prepared to hear that he does not approve of them – she has drawn from childhood and has had very little teaching. But if Mrs Trotter could have Mr Ruskin's opinion, it would be most valuable.'

The note was delivered by a maid to the great man. When John Ruskin read it he nearly went into a sulk.

'I'm in Italy!' he moaned. 'And I don't want to spend my holiday being polite to English mothers who think that their very average daughters are very great artists. In any case, great artists are all men, not women.'

Despite feeling cross, John Ruskin decided to be polite and sent a letter back asking to see some of Lilias's paintings.

The young woman struggled to decide which ones to send and then gave a few to the maid. Imagine how she felt knowing that the greatest art critic in England was looking at her work. After what seemed a long time the maid knocked at her door and handed in a letter. It was an invitation to Lilias to go out sketching with John Ruskin!

Next day, with her sketchpad, pencils and watercolour paints neatly packed, Lilias set off, along with her mother and John Ruskin, to the lovely Abbey of San Gregorio.

'Draw that, Miss Trotter,' he said.

Lilias looked at the Abbey. It was very beautiful.

'Not the Abbey,' the artist told her. 'Draw that piece of marble.'

Lilias looked at the marble and then looked more closely. At first it seemed just grey stone but, after a few minutes, the young woman could see veins of different colours and changes in the texture of the stone. Mr Ruskin was pleased to see that his new pupil didn't rush to draw or paint but sat looking at her subject for some time before starting. What Lilias perhaps didn't know at the time was that John Ruskin had written a whole book called 'Stones of Venice.' He was a real expert!

That day was very special for Lilias but it was very special for the great artist too. Before then he'd thought that women couldn't paint or draw as well as men. And he'd told his students that too. They were all men! Later, in a lecture he gave in Oxford, this is what he said about his very first meeting with Lilias Trotter.

'For a long time I used to say ... that, except in a graceful and minor way, women could not paint or draw. I am beginning to bow myself to the much more delightful conviction that no one else can. ... When I was in Venice in 1876 ... two English ladies, mother and daughter, were staying at the same hotel. One day the mother sent me a pretty note asking if I would look at the young lady's drawings. On my somewhat sulky permission a few were sent, in which I saw there was extremely right minded and careful work ... I sent back a request that the young lady might be allowed to come out sketching with me. ... She seemed to learn everything the instant she was shown it.'

What a holiday that turned out to be. The famous John Ruskin took Mrs Trotter and Lilias all over Venice, telling them the history of the city as they went from place to place.

'Today we are going along the Grand Canal,' he told them one morning. 'And you'll sketch as we go.'

There was no time for long looks at things as their gondola went along the canal, and John Ruskin was delighted to see that his young friend was able to do quick sketches very accurately.

The following day dawned sunny. 'Today is perfect for the Piazzetta and the Square of St Mark,' the women were told.

Lilias felt as if she was walking on air. She'd only had a few art lessons as a child and here she was, being taken on a sketching tour of one of the most beautiful cities in the world by one of the best artists in the world. If she thought she was dreaming, she was wrong!

John Ruskin had a studio in Venice and he took the two women to see it.

'Do you recognise that painting?' he asked.

Lilias had spent many, many hours in art galleries and reading books about art history. She knew that the painting Mr Ruskin was working on was a copy of one called St Ursula's Dream by Carpaccio. He allowed her to examine his work very carefully, to see the angles of his brush strokes and how he mixed his colours. It was like a university course for her!

You Don't Like Purple!

Back home in London, Lilias was soon at work at the Welbeck Street Institute, but she had other ideas too.

'I was thinking,' she said to her sister Emily, and then she fell silent.

'And are you going to share your thinking or just leave me hanging here?' laughed Emily.

Lilias smiled.

'It's just an idea. I don't know if anything could come of it, but ...' There was a pause while she sorted out her thoughts. 'You know that at Welbeck Street we look after the young women and do what we can for them. Well, just a few streets away there are different kinds of girls and women and perhaps we could do something for them too.'

'Who do you mean?' Emily puzzled.

'I'm thinking of the business women who work in the high-class shops in Regent Street and Oxford Street and those who work for the trading houses. They don't need cheap housing, but perhaps we could give them something that they do need. Do you think we might hold meetings for them too, meetings where we could talk about Jesus and study the Bible.'

Emily was quiet for a little while. That was a feature of Lilias and her sisters. They didn't rush into speaking before they worked out what they wanted to say.

'I'm sure meetings like that would be a real help to them, and they'd enjoy them too, I imagine,' said Emily. 'But I can't think where you'd meet. These girls wouldn't feel comfortable going to the Welbeck Street Institute and they'd probably not want to go to a church hall unless it was their own church. You know what people are like.'

'I know that,' Lilias agreed. 'But I was thinking of having meetings in homes, in our drawing room, for example.'

Now, before you think that every large house in Britain had a room especially for people to draw in, they didn't then and they certainly don't now! In the 16th Century grand houses had a room that the owners and their guests could withdraw (go out) to for privacy from other people in the house. It was then called the withdrawing room and the name was shortened to drawing room over the years.

Emily and her sister talked for a long time and decided that Lilias's idea could work. A little group of young women investigated the high-class businesses and shops in central London and found out who worked where. Then they sent invitations to 'drawing room meetings' or 'at homes' in the Trotters' house in Montagu Square. Young women and some older women too, went along. Perhaps some went just to see the inside of a lovely house. Maybe others went because they thought the invitations were very kind. And I'm sure that a few went along because they were lonely and hoped to make new friends. Whatever brought them, all the women who attended heard about the Lord Jesus in the relaxed surroundings of the Trotters' own home.

If that all sounds deadly serious and boring, here is what someone wrote about 40 Montagu Square: 'That unique household where Lily lived with her mother and brother and sisters, was a place of sunny gladness and laughter ....' You'll notice that Lilias was called Lily. That was her pet name.

Some friends of Lilias and her sisters also went to the meetings and very soon those who came from the shops and other businesses felt part of a very happy group of young women. Some people seem to think that they can only talk about God in a very serious voice and that he disapproves of laughter and happiness. What they forget is that God, who made all things, made laughter and happiness too!

When John Ruskin returned to England from Venice, he did not forget about Lilias. In fact, they wrote to each other often and sometimes he asked her to send drawings and paintings for him to look at. One set of six paintings done on a holiday in Norway were framed by him and shown to his students in Oxford. That was despite having told them before he met the Trotters that women could never draw or paint as well as men! When he showed them the Norwegian paintings, Mr Ruskin told his students that they were 'exactly what we should all like to be able to do.' That was one big compliment!

Not only did John Ruskin and Lilias write letters, but they became visitors to each other's homes. Mr Ruskin invited Lilias to visit him in the Lake District and she went there from time to time with her mother or with one of her brothers or sisters. When Mrs Trotter first wrote her note to John Ruskin you might remember he was in rather a sulk about having to be polite about Lilias's paintings. Things must have changed. Here's what he wrote the day before he was expecting Lilias and her sister Margaret to arrive at Brantwood, his splendid home overlooking Coniston Water.

'I am ready for you both this minute, if you could only come! Oh dear, I'm afraid it's going to rain tomorrow, and now – it's exquisite. But rain or cloud, it will still be beautiful – the woods are in such glory, and laburnum and hawthorn at their best – not a rose out yet – you will watch them through all their sweet lives. Love to Margaret. Her room is little but close to your turret, and she can skip across in the early morning.'

That doesn't sound in the least sulky!

'We're nearly there!' Lilias said, as their carriage trundled along the road the day after that letter was written.

To their right was a steep tree-covered hillside and to their left the hill continued downwards to the lake. As they turned a corner a road went off to the right and climbed steeply upwards.

'There's Brantwood,' Lilias laughed. 'We're here!'

Before their carriage reached the front of the cream-coloured three-storey house, John Ruskin flung open the door and rushed out to welcome his guests.

'It's not raining after all,' said Margaret. 'Just look at that view!'

They stood for a few minutes as the coachman talked to the horses. They were very happy to stop as the road had been hilly.

'That's the Old Man of Coniston,' Mr Ruskin told Margaret, pointing to the mountain on the other side of the lake. 'And you wouldn't have been able to see it earlier because of the rain. I told the sun to come out to welcome you, and it has!'

As soon as Margaret and Lilias had taken off their coats and bonnets they were shown into the drawing room and served Indian tea. No lady would have gone out without a bonnet in the 1880s!

'I love this room,' smiled Lilias. 'It feels like home.'

John Ruskin sat back in his chair and smiled. 'What do you like about it?' he asked.

As usual the young woman thought before she answered and, anyway, she was ready for her tea!

'I like that painting,' she told him, pointing to a picture of Mr Ruskin as a three-year-old boy, wearing a flowing white dress tied with a blue ribbon that matched his light blue shoes. The shoes were also tied with blue ribbons. Fashions have certainly changed since John wore that dress in 1822!

Margaret rose and went to look at his shell collection that was laid out in a tall cabinet.

'These are beautiful,' she commented.

Her sister looked from the shells to the collections of stones beside them.

'I like the stones,' Lilias told John Ruskin. 'They remind me of the piece of marble you asked me to sketch when we first met in Venice.'

Later on in their visit to Brantwood, Lilias and Margaret were discussing their favourite colours.

'I don't like purple,' said Lilias. 'I don't know why, but I would never wear anything purple.'

Margaret didn't have time to reply for John Ruskin jumped to his feet.

'You don't like purple!' he gasped, amazed at the very idea.

Lilias and Margaret just looked at each other as their friend went from one cabinet in the room to another taking out things to prove what he was about to say. Within ten minutes the square table in the middle of the room was almost covered with purple things and books that he took from the glass-fronted bookcase beside the fire.

'Look at this,' he said, handing Lilias a chunk of amethyst about the size of a small loaf of bread. 'Take it to the window and really look at it,' ordered Mr Ruskin. 'Imagine that amethyst had eyes and then look it in the eyes and tell it you don't think that it's beautiful.'

Lilias went to the window and looked at the thing she held in her hands. She needed both hands for it was so heavy! As she stood by the window the sun's rays hit the amethyst and it shone like a pale purple diamond. The light danced on it as she moved the stone this way and that. Doing what she often did, Lilias just looked … and looked … and looked for what seemed to Margaret a long, long time.

'It's beautiful,' Lilias said softly. 'It is absolutely beautiful.'

Mr Ruskin busied himself at the table, finding the pages he was looking for in books and leaving them open in front on him.

'Now come here,' he told his young friend. 'Look at these amethysts, every one of them is a different shade of purple, every single one of them is absolutely beautiful. And these rock crystals, are they not lovely too?'

Lilias had to agree. She had lost the battle for purple already and John Ruskin still had more, much more, to say and show her.

'Sit down and look at these,' he said to both young women.

As the three of them sat round the table he took book after book and pointed at the pictures of paintings.

'What would the great artist John Turner have done without purple?' he asked, showing them scenes with purple mountains and sunsets with purple streaks across gold and orange skies.'

'You're quite right,' Lilias said. 'I was wrong.'

'And look at these birds,' he told her, showing her paintings by William Hunt. 'The birds have purple in them and you say you don't like purple. When you paint birds, are you going to change them to colours that you happen to like?'

The battle was over. The lesson was done. If you are ever able to see paintings done by Lilias over her long life, you'll discover that purple featured like all the other colours. She painted what she saw in front of her, not what she wanted things to look like.

A Big Decision

Over the years Mrs Trotter's health had not been good. Although she was not an old woman, she had little strength and energy. The doctors decided that she had a heart condition and, because of that, she had to take things easy. Fortunately, there was a cook and house maids to look after her home, but, sadly, she died in 1878. Lilias missed her mother very much indeed, as they had been good friends. She missed her especially after a discussion with John Ruskin that made her think really, really hard.

'You are going to have to make up your mind,' he told her, when she was visiting his home in the Lake District.

Mr Ruskin and Lilias were sitting in his garden, and what a garden it was! It had been cut out of a very steep hillside and the path up to the top was a real climb. Sitting on a seat near the top of the garden, the pair of them looked over the lawn in front of the house and down the rugged hillside garden to Coniston Water, one of the deepest lakes in England. On the other side of the lake lay the village of Coniston with its white houses glistening in the sunshine. The Old Man of Coniston rose high behind the village, towering over all the other fells in the range.

'You could become the greatest living painter,' Ruskin said, to Lilias's absolute amazement. 'Your paintings would be treasured for ever.'

Lilias held her breath because she didn't know what to say. She was twenty-six years old and had just lost her mother. Now the man she respected as her teacher and friend was saying wonderful and impossible things.

'But,' went on Mr Ruskin, 'you will have to decide between all the other things you are doing and your art. You can't run your missions and spend your days helping people and study art as well. You have to really study art in order to become the great painter that is inside you.'

Lilias felt a shiver down her back despite the heat of the day.

When she discussed this with her friend back in London, she said, 'I need prayer to see God's way more clearly.'

The problem was that Lilias knew that it was God who had given her the gift of art. But she knew in her heart that God had also given her the gifts of loving and serving the women she helped in London. Would there be enough hours in each day to serve them and also to study and paint? Could she do both? In her diary Lilias wrote, 'I know God will make it all clear and not let me go wrong.'

It took time and prayer and patience, and John Ruskin had to be patient too. The young woman, who wouldn't rush into drawing a sketch without really looking at her subject, would not rush into making a decision that would affect her whole life. In May 1879, at Mr Ruskin's lovely home, Lilias knew what she should do.

'I see as clear as daylight now, I cannot give myself to painting in the way he means and continue still to "seek first the kingdom of God and his righteousness."'

John Ruskin was seriously disappointed and tried to persuade his friend to change her mind. He even wrote telling Lilias that he had a plan to open an art school for girls in London with her as the principal! But that was not to be. Lilias didn't give up drawing and painting, not at all, but it wasn't the most important thing in her life from that day on.

Back in London Lilias and her friends continued their work serving the women who worked in the city, both those who lived in the Welbeck Street Institute and those who came from the high-class shops and businesses to their drawing room meetings. But there was another group of young women that Lilias was concerned about. These were poor women who walked the streets of London earning money any way they could, sometimes by doing truly awful things. Many of them gathered in the area around Victoria Station, which was not a safe place to be.

Someone like Lilias would never have dreamed of going to that part of the city alone in the dark. But Lilias was different; she was right there with the poor women who needed her help. When she met the women she took them to a hostel where they could have a good night's sleep. The next morning they were told about good ways of earning money and how they could get out of the messes they were in. Once she was even able to stop a very troubled woman from killing herself.

Having worked really hard for some years, Lilias was worn out and ill. Because it was so long ago we don't know exactly what was wrong with her, but from then on her heart was weaker than normal. However, as soon as she was well she was back at work.

Lilias Trotter and her helpers seemed to have one idea after another. When they realised that there was nowhere cheap for women to eat, they opened a dining room at Welbeck Street, just for women. The hot meals that were served there cost them very little. Sometimes Lilias gathered in the money. 'It is fun sitting at the desk,' she wrote in her diary 'seeing pennies turn into shillings, and shillings into sovereigns on the busy days of the week.' Shillings and sovereigns don't exist now!

At the same time as the work in London continued to grow, there was often missionary news from overseas. Thirty years earlier an Englishman, called Hudson Taylor, went to China as a missionary.

'Have you heard that more than 165 men and women are going to join Hudson Taylor in China?' a friend asked Lilias.

'Yes,' she smiled. 'I heard that and I wish them very well. But there's enough work here in London to keep me busy all my life.'

'I'm sure you're right,' agreed her red-headed friend.

'A Ticket to Algiers, please'

In May 1887 something happened that proved both Lilias and her friend wrong. Lilias heard a missionary called Edward Glenny speaking about his work in North Africa. It was a Thursday evening and Mr Glenny started his talk by telling the audience that he had been in Algeria in North Africa the previous Sunday! Remember, this was in 1887 and there were no aircraft then!

If Algeria is as easy to get to as that,' Lilias thought, 'I could spend half the year there and the other half at home.'

God spoke to her through Edward Glenny that night and Lilias's heart was set on Algeria from that day on. At the end of the meeting the speaker said, 'Is there anyone in this room God is calling to North Africa?' And in her heart Lilias answered, 'It's me. God is calling me.'

Some months later she and her sister Jaqueline talked about the future.

'Are you very disappointed that the mission you applied to won't allow you to join them because of your weak heart?' Jaqueline asked.

Lilias thought for a minute. 'I was at first,' she admitted, 'but they have agreed that I can go to Algeria and work alongside them. I don't think they wanted to take me on as one of their missionaries because of my health. That would have been quite a responsibility.'

'And is that what you're going to do?'

'Yes,' said Lilias. 'It is. And I've arranged to do some months of training at Mildmay Hospital before we go.'

Jaqueline smiled. 'I'm really going to miss you. After all, you are my young sister.'

Laughing, Lilias reminded her that she was thirty-five years old!

The weeks that followed were very busy. Lilias and her dressmaker discussed what clothes should be made. Suitable shoes were bought and hats to guard against the sun. Of course, clothes were not the only things that needed to be prepared. Not knowing what would be available in Algiers, Lilias had to take all that she might need. The pile of books grew and grew. And, of course, there were her painting things. She couldn't forget any of them.

The 5th of March 1888 was a very special day. Lilias and her friend Lucy Lewis climbed aboard a train in London's Waterloo Station. A large group of women stood on the platform and sang a hymn to them as the train built up steam and began, very slowly at first, to chug out of the station. The train took the two women to Southampton where Blanche Haworth was waiting to join them. All three were on their way to Algeria. At Southampton the women boarded the paddle steamer that would take them on the next leg of their journey.

'I feel I know Algeria,' Blanche said, as the great paddles turned and kept them moving forward. 'But the truth is that I only know about it.'

'I know nothing about Algeria,' a woman they'd met in the boat said. 'Tell me about it.'

Blanche was very happy to do that, and Lilias and Lucy were right there to fill up any facts that she missed, or correct any that she got wrong.

'Algeria stretches along the south coast of the Mediterranean Sea and runs south right to the Sahara Desert. It's the second largest country in Africa,' said Blanche. 'Most people live in the strip of land along the coast,' she went on.

'That strip of land is about 100 miles from north to south,' Lucy added.

'South of that are the Atlas Mountains,' Blanche continued.

Her fellow passenger's face lit up. 'I've heard of them,' she smiled, feeling very pleased with herself.

The women talked on and on. There was plenty of time to talk on a sea voyage.

It was in the evening of 8th March that the ship neared the Algerian coast and the port of Algiers. Lilias sat down and began to write.

'The first peaks of land came into sight, dim and purple. ... We went below for a time. And on coming up again there was a far-stretching cluster of golden stars, the lights of Algiers!'

The following morning she took up her pen once again.

'I shall never forget the loveliness of our first sight out of our port-hole of the Arab town rising tier above tier in a flow of cream colour against the blue-grey western sky. The water glimmered in blue and gold below, and a flock of gulls sailed and wheeled between us and the land.'

Lilias, Blanche and Lucy had arrived. They were in Algeria! The three young women stood on the upper deck and sang the same hymn their friends had sung as their train left Waterloo Station in London just four days before. Now, here they were. It seemed like a world away. They knew nobody and did not speak a word of Arabic. If they were in the least worried, it certainly didn't show on their smiling, joyful faces!

Finding Their Way Around

As the three women disembarked from their ship a little crowd gathered round about them. Being a port city, they knew there was certain to be someone who could speak English, and there was. Before long a carriage had been found for them and they were hoisted aboard. Their luggage was put on beside them and they headed off to the lodgings at Pension Anglo Suisse that they had arranged by letter. No sooner were they in the door than one of them remembered that, allowing for the time difference, it was exactly the same time as a little group of their friends would be meeting to pray for them in England. Forgetting about their unpacking, they knelt down on their knees and prayed too.

The following day Lilias, Blanche and Lucy found their way to a church service held for English Christians living in Algiers or visiting the city. After the service, as the three young women set off for their lodgings, they left an interesting conversation behind them.

'Well,' said an elderly man, 'that was a surprise! We expected just the usual people here this morning and we found ourselves joined by three of the most enthusiastic young women I've ever met.'

His wife wasn't quite so sure. 'They look and sound as if they're from wealthy homes. I doubt they'll cope with the hardships of living in a place like this.'

But her husband didn't agree. 'It certainly won't be easy for them, but I think they know that. It's not as if they are holiday-makers hoping to tell people about Jesus for a fortnight and then go right back home again. They seem absolutely set on staying and being real long-term missionaries.'

'We'll see,' was all his wife would say. 'We'll just have to wait and see.'

Back at her lodgings, Lilias wrote down how she felt that day. 'I could cover sheets of paper if I tried to say how happy we are. My heart just goes out to, and claps round, the Arab people. We do love them.'

Lilias was good at putting words on paper, but she was even better at putting paint on paper and she was often to be found sketching new and interesting things in Algiers.

'That's exactly what it looked like!' Lucy laughed. 'You're painting the view of the mountains that we saw from the boat as we came into the harbour.'

Her friend agreed that was exactly what she was doing.

'I never want to forget it,' she said. 'It was like a dream coming true. We've looked forward to being here for so long. And we've prayed that God would bring us here safely. Now we are here I want a picture of it to remind me of how thankful I feel.'

Lucy giggled. 'And how excited!'

Smiling at her friend, who looked just like a teenager when she giggled, Lilias agreed that she too was very, very excited.

Each day Lilias, Blanche and Lucy went out for several walks in the city as they tried to find their way around. It was a place of great hustle and bustle. The streets were narrow, and people pushed against one other and squeezed past each other in a way that the three young women were certainly not used to in their polite parts of London.

'The men's white robes look very bright in the sun,' commented Lucy, as they walked along a street that was so narrow she could stand in the middle and touch the buildings on either side of it!

Lilias smiled. 'And it's as well they are white,' she said. 'For when you step into a narrow street like this one, the sun doesn't reach the road at all and you can hardly see a thing until your eyes get used to the dark.'

'Watch out!' Blanche said, pulling Lilias to the side. 'Let the water-carrier past.'

It was so dark that Lilias hadn't noticed a young man coming towards her with a full water jug balanced on his shoulder.

Blanche smiled at the water carrier who looked at the three strangers and broke into such a grin that they just wanted to hug him. But that would have toppled his water jar and given him the fright of his life!

'How I wish I could have spoken to the water-carrier,' said Lucy, when they reached their lodgings. 'But we don't know a single word of Arabic between us.'

'Not yet,' Blanche agreed, 'but we'll learn.'

'Yes, we will,' Lilias said, 'but the first thing we need to do is find a house for ourselves. We can only stay at the Pension Anglo Suisse for a short time.'

At the pension the young women met Mrs Kemp and her three daughters, the Misses Kemp, who were about the same age as them.

'We are living in a villa near here,' Mrs Kemp told them, 'but we come to the pension for our meals.'

Although hearing the Arabic language all around them was a real thrill to the three newcomers to Algiers, it was just great to have four English speakers there too!

'Would you like to come back to the villa with us?' asked Alice Kemp, after they'd had their meal. 'We have a little Bible study every week and it would be lovely if you could be there.'

The Kemp mother and daughters were Lilias, Blanche and Lucys' first friends in Algiers and they were Christians. God is SO good.

Like Playing Houses

The next few weeks were spent looking for a house to rent and, having arrived on 9th March, they moved into a flat in the French area of Algiers in May. At last they could unpack the wooden crates that contained their belongings. How did there come to be a French area in Algiers? It needs a short history lesson to understand that, so here goes.

In 1830 the French navy sailed into the port town of Algiers. King Charles X of France had ordered his navy to invade Algeria! For very complicated reasons there were a good number of abandoned buildings in the town. The sailors took over the buildings and settled there. Over the years that followed more and more French people came, for by then the country was under French rule. That's why parts of the city of Algiers were very French and why the French language was spoken in Algeria, especially in the north.

Even the geography of the city showed its history. Now, that may seem a very strange thing to say, but this is what I mean. In the French parts of Algiers were the bigger houses and bigger businesses. Then, inland and uphill, were the areas of the city lived in by Algerians and other people groups. These tended to be less well off. And further out, in the oldest part of Algiers, lived the Arab people. Their houses were often, but not always, quite poor.

It was the Arab people who tugged at the missionaries' hearts. God had called Lilias, Blanche and Lucy to be missionaries to them and they prayed he would open up ways of meeting them. The women decided on a prayer that they would all pray, and it was in three parts. Their prayer was that God would open up doors, that he would open up hearts and that he would open up heaven. What did they mean by heaven being opened? They were praying that God would send down blessings on the work they would do.

Over the next few months Lilias and her friends had one, and then another, and then yet another young girl to help them look after their new home. But each time something happened and things just didn't work out.

'I think we should just look after ourselves,' suggested Blanche. 'Doing our own shopping would help us to meet people.'

'That's true,' Lilias agreed. 'And it would make us more like the people who live round about us. Most of them don't have maids.'

'So that's decided!' said Lucy. 'We'll do our own shopping, cooking, cleaning and wash our own clothes.'

Now, this must seem a bit strange to most of you who are reading this story. But making up a rota for doing their own cleaning, washing, shopping and so on was really rather like making up the rules of a game to Lilias, Lucy and Blanche. None of them had ever done a washing, for they'd all had laundry maids at home.

Cooking was entirely new to them. Just try to imagine what some of the first meals might have tasted like! And shopping for ingredients in a strange town, even if they were in the French quarter, must have been interesting, to say the least. Lilias wrote, 'Blanche proved to be a good cook and I was the house and parlour maid. Lucy took turns at helping us.'

The three adventurers hardly had time to settle in their new home when a telegram arrived for Lilias. People only sent telegrams when there was urgent (and often bad) news. No doubt she prayed as she unfolded the sheet of paper. Inside was the news that her much-loved sister Jaqueline had died.

The young woman sat down. Her friends knew immediately that something was far wrong and were so sorry to hear the news.

'I thought she was getting better after her operation,' Lucy said quietly.

Lilias nodded. 'Yes, everyone did, and it wasn't serious surgery, as far as we knew.'

She was quiet for a few minutes, thinking of her sister and remembering all sorts of things.

'Let's pray,' said Blanche, and she did.

Tears rolled down Lilias's cheeks as she thought of never seeing Jaqueline again until they met in heaven.

'She's with Jesus,' she said. 'And that is so much better than being here on earth. Imagine my dear sister seeing Jesus face-to-face.'

As it was a Sunday, the three young women had time to talk to each other. Lilias thought out loud, 'My idea was to live here in Algiers for most of each year and to go back to London to be with Jaqueline for the rest of each year,' she said to her friends. 'But I don't need to do that now. I can stay here all year round and really make this my home.'

The three young women were living on their own money and gifts from people who supported them. That allowed them the freedom to live in Algeria most of the year and to go back to England for some months every summer. Now, with Jaqueline's death, it was beginning to look as if God might want them there all the time.

'We'll have to think about this and pray about it,' Lucy said. 'And there's no hurry to make decisions for we only just arrived three months ago.'

A few hours after hearing about her sister's death, Lilias went with her friends to the English church in the city where people cared for her with great kindness.

Learning Arabic

By this time all three of them had a little smattering of the Arabic language. They knew the names of most of the things they had to buy in the market each day and were able to make polite comments to people they met in the streets, the smiling young water-carriers among them.

Lilias wrote to a friend back in England about their language study.

'We are using the Bible to teach us Arabic, starting with the first chapter of John's Gospel. We are learning new words, one at a time. The Gospel begins, 'In the beginning was the Word, and the Word was with God, and the Word was God.' So the first word we learned was 'In' and then 'the'. And do you know what was really exciting? When we'd learned the word 'Word' and then came across it just half a line later, and then again in the next line. It sounds funny, but it was really good to come to a word we'd already learned. We felt as if we were getting somewhere!'

The three missionaries spent long hours with their Bibles and their Arabic dictionaries. After a while they joined an Arabic class and that helped them along, but only for a short time.

'It's so disappointing that the class has been stopped,' Lucy said, as they walked home together.

Blanche agreed. 'When our teacher is better the class will start up again, I'm sure.'

It did, but in the meantime they paid a young Arab boy to come to their home to read to them. He came three evenings one week and three the next and he could never have had more serious students than Lilias, Lucy and Blanche. But after a fortnight the boy didn't come back. He was a Muslim and not at all comfortable about being in the home of three Christian missionaries.

'We need to get a real teacher or it's going to take us years to learn the language,' Blanche said.

Her friends agreed. Right away they started to look for a suitable person whose Arabic was good, who was a patient teacher and who wouldn't mind being with Christians. That's how they met Mr Fabsal, who proved to be just right for them.

As soon as the women could speak a little Arabic they put it to good use.

'How are we going to tell our neighbours about Jesus?' was the question they kept asking each other.

'Well,' said Lilias, 'between us we have enough words to give short talks if we write them out beforehand and learn them by heart. Do you agree?'

Her friends nodded their heads.

'And we've enough space here to hold meetings,' they decided.

'But how do we get people to come?' was the next question.

They decided to make leaflets that they could give to those they met in the streets around their home. They had a machine that allowed them to make copies because this was in the days before computers and printers. Lilias, the artist of the group, wrote an invitation and some Bible verses on a sheet of paper and drew a lovely border around the edge. The sheet was then copied. After that all three women sat at the table and coloured in the border round the invitations. They looked lovely!

'How do you say, "Can you read in Arabic?" they asked Mr Fabsal, before he started their next lesson.

After he left that day, they prayed together and then went out into the streets. Knocking on each door, they asked the person who answered, 'Can you read?' If the answer was 'yes', they gave one of their beautifully coloured invitations.

The first meeting in their home was on a Sunday. The room had been cleaned, lamps hung on the walls and chairs laid out neatly. Blanche, who played the harmonium, was ready to teach some songs. More than twenty people arrived and the three women, who had learned everything off by heart in Arabic, each said their piece. There was singing, Bible reading and prayer. The missionaries were delighted ... but not so delighted when nobody at all turned up at the next two meetings. After that people began to come in ones and twos and they felt that their missionary work had really begun.

Lilias wrote in her diary what a typical day was like.
'Our servant girl comes about 6 am.' (They must have decided not to do all the housework and cooking themselves after a while!) 'She makes our breakfast of coffee and bread and leaves it on the kitchen table for us. We collect our meal and take it back to our rooms

where we stay until 8.30 when we meet to read the Bible and pray. That takes till 9.15. From then until 10.30 we do little bits of housework and write letters before beginning our Arabic lessons for the day.

At 12 noon we have lunch and then a short time of prayer before our siesta. Teatime is 3.30 and then we go out into the town with our invitations. We're home by 6 pm when we have a little to eat, wash up the dishes and read and write letters until we have cocoa and go off to bed at 10 pm.'

Things seemed to go well for a time but then came a problem. Some local people who wanted to cause trouble came along to the meetings and tried to spoil them. Most of them were French boys in their teens and they really were pests. They came looking for trouble and brought trouble with them. Those were difficult days for the three women who had never met anyone like them. Of course, some came because they wanted to learn about Jesus. So they stopped coming when they couldn't hear over the noise. The meetings were hard work but Lilias, Blanche and Lucy were there to work hard, and they did.

However, Lucy wasn't really strong and the climate began to affect her health. It was with sad hearts that her two friends had to say goodbye to her when it was decided that, for the sake of her health, Lucy would have to go home to England.

The Wordless Book

A few months later, on New Year's Day 1889, Lilias and Blanche held an afternoon tea for a very unlikely set of guests. They invited the young men who worked as water-carriers in the town!

'What would they most like to eat?' Blanche wondered, over and over again. In the end they provided what must have seemed like a feast to the young men. They had fresh fruit, dried fruit and nuts, hard-boiled eggs, bread and home-made jam and other things besides. The young men, some of them really just boys, ate like they'd not eaten for a week! When there were only crumbs on the table Blanche sat down at her harmonium and started to play a tune. Before long everyone was singing together.

After the last song, Lilias got to her feet.

'I have something to show you,' she told their guests. 'It is a book, a very special book.'

And before any of them could point out that they couldn't read, she went on, 'This book is special because it doesn't have any words in it.'

The young men looked puzzled. They didn't know much about books, but they did know that all books had words in them.

Lilias held up the little book. Each page was a different colour. There was a black page followed by a red one. Then came a white page followed by a green one. Last of all there was a shiny golden page.

'The black page tells us about our hearts,' Lilias explained. 'Every single person has a black heart because we've all done wrong and sinful things.' Then she told them how Jesus died on the cross to wash away the sins of all who trust in him. 'The red page reminds us of the blood of Jesus shed on the cross. And the white page shows us that our sins are washed away and our hearts made clean, if we are truly sorry and ask Jesus to forgive us.'

'What does the green page say?' one of the boys asked.

'Green is the colour of growing,' said Lilias. 'And the green page shows us that, after we are forgiven, we grow more like Jesus every day, if we learn what the Bible says and pray to God our father.'

The oldest water-carrier wanted to know about the golden page.

Lilias smiled. 'The golden page is very special,' she told them. 'The golden page tells us about heaven where all Christians go when they die. Everything in heaven is glorious and perfect and there is nothing bad, nothing sad, nothing sore and nobody becomes ill or dies there. And, best of all, the Lord Jesus is in heaven with his people.'

One of the boys grinned. 'Gold is a good colour for that page,' he said.

He was right.

After that Lilias played a game with their guests. She called out a colour – either black, white, red, green or gold – and asked what it meant. Before they left that afternoon, all the young men knew the complete story of the wordless book, even if they couldn't read one single word of print!

That was the first time that Lilias had used the wordless book in Algiers but it certainly wasn't the last. She used it over and over again during her lifetime in Algeria. And it has been used, and is still being used, by missionaries all over the world.

The special thing about the wordless book is that it can be used whatever language people speak. Not only that but, when people have had the colours explained to them, they can 'read' the colours of the book themselves even if they can't actually read at all!

It was boys and young men who visited the missionaries' home that day. Some time later Lilias and Blanche agreed to have a special tea for girls who worked in factories in the city. When not a single girl turned up, the women went out into the streets and invited forty Arab boys to come instead. Most of them worked in the local market-place or cleaned people's shoes. They went along, enjoyed their tea, and kept on coming. Twelve of them came weekly to a Bible class. The girls never knew what they missed!

In 1890 Lilias and Blanche went to England for some months and that became a feature of their lives. They worked very hard in Algiers and then rested and recovered in England before going back. The two women became three when Helen Freeman arrived to join them. Helen and Lilias had worked together in London and they were great friends. The three missionaries – Lilias, Blanche and Helen – were to spend the rest of their lives in Algeria. That's how much they loved the Arab people.

No sooner were the women settled in again when the boys' Bible study was restarted. One young man, his name was Ahmed, was especially pleased about that because he had become a Christian.

Ahmed suffered badly for trusting in Jesus. More than once he arrived at the missionaries' door battered and bruised and covered in blood. Things were so hard for him that Lilias and Blanche arranged for Ahmed to go to another city for a while. Becoming a Christian often meant trouble for new Christians at that time in Algiers.

When the missionaries went out into the city they rarely met any women. Men and boys thronged the streets but women were strangely absent.

'How can we get to know women?' asked Helen, after she'd been in Algiers for a time. 'They are all stuck in their houses and courtyards. We can't get to them and, even if they know about our work, they can't get to us.'

The three friends thought about the problem.

'I think that the only thing we can do is try to get to know the children who play in the streets and hope that they invite us home,' Blanche suggested.

Lilias agreed. 'Maybe if we make friends with the boys and girls, they'll tell their mothers about us.'

And that's exactly what happened.

Would you like to know how women lived in Algeria then? Well, they lived behind locked doors. Nobody could get in to them from the street. But behind the locked doors there were courtyards and open spaces where the women and older girls walked about freely and lived happy lives. Four or five families lived behind one door. They weren't crushed together. Each family had its own space.

Men were not meant to go where the women were between 7 am and 7 pm. This was because they had strict rules about men meeting women who did not belong to their family. If a man did have to go in, he coughed so loudly that all the women heard him and scurried into the shadows until he went out again. When the men came home after 7 pm, all the women stayed in their own parts of the building until morning.

By getting to know the children the three missionaries found themselves invited to meet their mums. It wasn't at all unusual for Lilias, Blanche and Helen to be let in through a street door and then to separate and visit the women of different families in their own rooms or courtyards. Many of them were interested in the stories they told them about Jesus. The visitors took tiny gifts with them – sweets, pictures, little cards with Bible verses written on them and home-made gifts like pin cushions.

If women could read, and very few of them could, they loved to get story books about Jesus which they read and then passed on to their friends. As time went on the missionaries' Arabic improved. And, of course, the more Arabic people they spoke to the better they learned to speak the language. Learning the language was really hard work but they were beginning to see that it was well worth it.

Since arriving in the city of Algiers, the three women had used the French they learned from their governesses to talk to French-speaking people who lived in the city. They even held meetings in French. Eventually they passed on that work to other people and concentrated on what they believed God had called them to do. Of course, there were Arab people in the countryside as well as in the city and it was to hillside villages that Lilias began to turn her eyes.

New Arrivals

After some time two more missionaries came out to join them. They were Francis and Reba Brading, a young couple from England. Having more people meant that the work in the city could go on as usual even if two missionaries went out to visit the country villages. Not surprisingly Lilias was the first to go, along with her friend Blanche. In March 1893 the pair of them set off on a real adventure.

If Blanche wrote a letter to a friend in England, it might have read something like this.

'The first part of the journey was by train, all 288 miles of it! Then we climbed aboard a horse-drawn cart for the next 150 miles. Now, when I say a horse-drawn cart, that's exactly what I mean. It wasn't the kind of stagecoach you are used to.'

'Eventually we reached El Kantara, which is called the gateway to the desert. It is sandy before El Kantara, but real desert after it. And it really is like a gateway because we had to travel through a deep gorge that grew narrower as we went through it until the sides were only about 45 metres apart. Suddenly we were out of the gorge into a valley filled with palm trees. In the far distance were the most amazing purple mountains.

Lilias, as you can imagine, was busy with her paints. Perhaps you'll see what it looks like one day when you look at one of her lovely paintings.'

Blanche and Lilias were very unusual travellers in that part of Algeria where most people had never seen European women. One day Lilias's hat was taken off by a curious Arab woman who wanted to see what her hair looked like. And she wanted to see what it felt like too so, having taken off the missionary's hat, she then went on to stroke her well-brushed smooth hair!

'Look at the skin on their hands!' another woman whispered to her friend. 'They don't have hands like our hands.'

They did really, but Lilias and Blanche were both wearing gloves!

The women still had another thirty miles to go after El Kantara and this part of the journey was done on camelback. Soon the palm trees were behind them and they were in real desert land with only a few palms here and there in the distance. As they passed through villages they dismounted from their camels and talked with anyone who would talk with them. Then, at long last, the travellers reached Biskra, their destination.

Although Lilias had decided not to be a full-time artist, she was never without her sketchbook and watercolour paints. That journey can be read in both words and paintings in her diary.

The next day Blanche went in one direction and Lilias went in the other. They had decided to explore Biskra's narrow streets and to meet the people who lived there.

Some children skipped along the road and stopped right in front of Lilias. One little boy came up behind them, limping as he went. Crouching down to their level, the missionary began to talk to the children.

'What's your name?' she asked the little boy with the limp.

'Ahmed,' said the boy.

Lilias smiled. The name Ahmed was special to her as the very first person to become a Christian through their work in Algiers was called Ahmed.

'Are these your brothers and sisters?' she asked.

Ahmed shook his head. 'My sister is at home. She has red eyes. My eyes are a little bit red too.'

The missionary looked at the boy's eyes and saw that he was telling the truth.

'Will you take me to your mother?' she asked. 'I would like to see your sister who has red eyes.'

Suddenly Ahmed lost all his shyness and grabbed Lilias's hand.

'My home is this way,' he said, importantly.

Lilias followed the little boy along the narrow road between the houses. She could see that Ahmed was delighted to be doing such an important job as taking a European woman to his home. The other boys and girls, who were a little envious, tagged along behind them. They had no intention of missing out on anything that was going on.

Dropping Lilias's hand when they reached the corner of his road, Ahmed ran ahead to tell his mother that they had a visitor. You would think that an Arab woman might be shy of meeting her very first European. But she wasn't. The village women knew about the missionary because news had already travelled through the village about the strange visitors. Lilias was hardly in the door when she was surrounded by chattering women and, before long, she was also surrounded by food. Although the village people didn't have much, they wanted to share what they had with her.

Before leaving, the missionary asked to see Ahmed's little sister who had red eyes. Not only were her eyes red, they were also sticky and sore. Lilias carried some simple medicines with her and clean boiled cloths too. She asked the woman how she was treating the problem. Lilias showed her how to dissolve a little salt in freshly boiled water and then let it cool before wiping the child's eyes with a clean cloth dipped in the salty water.

'Just wipe the eye once and then take a new cloth, dip it in the salty water and wipe the other eye. Try not to use the same cloth more than once and never use the same cloth for both eyes,' she explained. 'That just takes the infection from one eye to the other.'

The woman nodded and smiled.

'But I don't have so many clean clothes,' she admitted.

Lilias smiled. 'You just need two because you can wash them thoroughly after you've cleaned her eyes. They'll dry in the sun before you need them again.'

The missionary then cleaned Ahmed's eyes too and gave his mother the dirty cloths to wash and keep for next time.

Some women sat around the room and watched all that was going on.

'Would you like me to tell you a story?' asked Lilias.
Of course they would!

Once again she took out the wordless book and coloured page by coloured page she told the story of Jesus. At first the women looked puzzled. Because most of them couldn't read, the idea of a book wasn't one they were used to. And for the one or two who could read the idea of a book with no words was just plain strange. But before long they were listening to every word.

Later that day Blanche and Lilias talked over what they had done.

'It seems that our way to reach village women is through their children, just as it is in the city,' Lilias said. 'Otherwise they are firmly behind closed doors.'

Blanche nodded. 'That's true. But the children are happy to take us to their homes and sometimes we get such a warm welcome.'

'I certainly did today,' smiled her friend.

'It's good that we can give simple medical help too,' Blanche added. 'But what do you say when you are asked what you want?'

Lilias thought for a minute before answering. 'I usually say that I love the Arab people and want to tell them a story.'

While Ahmed's mother had welcomed her visitor warmly, that didn't always happen. Sometimes women were afraid in case their husbands would hear about it. And, if they'd heard from their friends that the visitors to the village were Christian missionaries, occasionally they shooed them away, telling them that Mohammed is the one who saves and that Allah is God. When that happened Lilias and Blanche knew not to argue. Instead they said goodbye graciously and moved on.

'Why is it that there are so few women to be seen in Algiers?' a visitor asked one day.

It took Blanche a minute to work out how to answer.

'Here are the facts,' she began. 'When girls are young, up to about ten years old, they have quite relaxed lives, though they don't ever have as much freedom as boys their own age. But when they reach ten, and begin to wear the veil that Muslim women have to wear, things change.'

'In what ways do they change?' the visitor wanted to know.

'In every way,' admitted Blanche. 'From then on they are rarely outside their own homes and courtyards, and their whole lives are spent pleasing their fathers. When they grow up, their fathers arrange marriages for them. Then, after they are married, they move to their husband's homes and are virtually prisoners there for the rest of their lives.'

'That's terrible!' the shocked visitor said.

Blanche knew she wasn't explaining it too well.

'The thing is that the girls don't know any different. For us that would be like being in prison. But they are proud of how things are. It can seem to them as though their fathers are protecting them and then their husbands take over their protection.'

'You mean they are happy living like that?'

'I think many of them are,' Blanche admitted, 'especially the older women. But when things go wrong, they can go horribly wrong.'

'What do you mean?'

'Well,' said Blanche, 'men often marry more than one woman. And sometimes, actually quite often, men decide they are tired of their older wives and divorce them.'

The visitor was shocked when she heard that. 'That's why you need to tell them about Jesus, men as well as women, and children too. He's the only one who can change their lives.'

Blanche agreed, and added, 'We want them to believe in Jesus so that they will, one day, go to heaven, not just so that they can have freedom to go outside.'

Home!

It was nearly six weeks from when they left Algiers that a telegram arrived. This time it was good news rather than bad. Their friends back in the city had found a suitable building for them to live in and work from. It was time for Blanche and Lilias to turn round and make the long journey home from Biskra by camel, cart and train. Of course, they didn't pack away the wordless book or some little books in Arabic that they'd brought with them. Those were the tools of their trade. They continued their missionary work in every village they went through, making sure that they visited different villages from those they'd been to on their outward journey.

What a welcome Lilias and Blanche had from their friends in Algiers and what a lot of catching up they had to do, but that had to wait. There were important things to discuss.

'Tell us about the house,' said Blanche, as soon as they sat down to drink tea.

Francis and Reba smiled at each other.

'I'm not sure that house is quite the right word,' grinned Reba, and then left her husband to tell the story.

'It's 2 Rue du Croissant, and it's a big building right in the Arab quarter of the city.'

Lilias liked the sound of that.

'It's really more like a small castle than a house,' Francis explained.

His wife laughed. 'It's more like a badger set than either a castle or a house!'

'How many rooms does it have?' Blanche wanted to know.

'We think there are twenty-five,' said Francis, 'but that includes a mosque, stables for horses and rooms that are not really rooms at all, just ways of getting from rooms to other ones.'

Lilias and Blanche looked at each other and smiled.

'This we have to see!' announced Lilias.

Blanche laughed. 'And soon!'

The two desert wanderers went with their friends to visit 2 Rue du Croissant. Lilias, who had the eye of an artist, took in every small detail as they walked there for the first time. It was right in the Arab part of town where the streets were so narrow they nearly touched each other at roof level. Rue du Croissant was a long street, but not the kind of street you think of today because sometimes it changed into being a flight of steps! You certainly couldn't have cycled or taken a car along it, but that didn't matter as cars hadn't been invented!

When they reached the house there was another set of stairs and then a solid wooden door, like a medieval castle door, with metal studs in it. And all of those interesting things were before they actually went into the house that was to become their home!

Francis opened the door and then he stood back to let Lilias and Blanche go in to the entrance hall. There was a hush as they took in the size of the place, and the sheer quirkiness of it. From the moment she went through the studded door, Lilias Trotter knew, deep inside herself, that she had come home.

'What fun our children will have playing hide and seek here,' Reba said, as they went from corridor to corridor, up and down stairs, in and out of rooms and more rooms and windowless rooms that, right enough, did only seem to be there to join the other rooms together.

'It's like a maze!' laughed Blanche, when they'd gone through it all, or perhaps hadn't. It was so hard to tell.

Lilias looked around. In her mind's eye she could picture 2 Rue du Croissant as their home and the centre of their work in Algiers as well as being the headquarters of their trips out to the desert villages.

'It's perfect,' Lilias said to the others. 'It is absolutely lovely. We'll be happy here and so will the Arab people who'll come to see us and to learn about the Lord Jesus.'

They looked around at the dust and the rubble and smiled.

'You can tell who the artists are,' Blanche told her friends. 'They have very vivid imaginations!'

In May 1893, Lilias and her fellow-workers moved into their new home.

'It's right away from the French part of Algiers,' Blanche said, as they looked out of a window. 'And it looks and feels very different.'

Lilias agreed. 'I love the narrow streets and winding passages. You just never know what you'll find next.'

Blanche laughed 'The first time we visited this house I wondered if I'd be able to find it again. There

77

were so many corners to go round. And that was out in the streets. When we came inside to explore I knew I could even get lost inside it. And I have done, several times!'

Men came and went, they walked and talked.

'What a busy place,' Blanche thought aloud.

Lilias smiled. 'This may sound strange,' she said to her friend. 'But at last I feel we are real missionaries to the Arab people, now that we are living right among them.'

Blanche laughed. 'It doesn't sound strange at all. That's exactly how I feel too!'

The Rue du Croissant was such a narrow street that if one of the missionaries opened an upstairs front window and stretched out her arm as far as she could, she could touch fingers with an Arab woman on the other side of the street, if she stretched out her hand. That's narrow!

Lilias and her friends were a great source of interest to the women who were their neighbours.

'Why are they here?' they asked each other.

'Why don't they live in better parts of the city with all the other Europeans?'

The women asked so many WHYS. If they ever asked Lilias and her friends, they were told that they were there to tell them about Jesus.

A few weeks after moving to their new home, the summer heat hit the city and that always drained Lilias's energy badly. She knew it was time to go back to England for a change of climate. Her feelings were all mixed up as she did her packing.

'Just when we're really getting settled into the Arab quarter of Algiers I'm packing up and going away. That feels strange,' she admitted, to her fellow-missionaries.

One of them looked at Lilias seriously.

'Do you think that, if you stayed, you'd be fit to work by the end of the summer heat?' she asked.

Lilias, who was as honest with herself as she was with her friends, knew that was right. If she didn't go back to England to build up her strength, she would be poorly by the end of the summer and no help at all with the mission.

It was a much better looking Lilias who arrived back at Rue du Croissant that October. Blanche and Helen, Lilias, Francis and Reba were delighted to be together again and they had so much catching up to do. No doubt the Brading children were pleased too!

'Does it feel good to be back?' Reba asked her friend.

Lilias smiled. 'It feels like I've come home,' she answered. 'It's a wonderful feeling.'

And it was quite true. Lilias's heart was no longer in London, it was in Algeria with the Arab people she loved so much. Of course, after three months away all she wanted to do was tell them that Jesus loved them and that he was the one and only Saviour.

Although she was glad to be back in Algiers, Lilias was already planning to leave again!

'I believe that God wants us to go back to Biskra and to explore what work we could do from there.'

This was no surprise to her friends. The four of them had been praying about this over the summer, for they knew how much Lilias longed to go to the villages.

'We can spend the winter planning a mission trip,' Blanche said. And they did.

Many times over that winter a map of Algeria lay on the table for them to talk about, pray over and plan for.

Winter in Algiers passed in the busiest way. The missionaries held classes for boys and girls and discussed the Lord Jesus with the menfolk out in the streets. They visited women in their homes and talked to them for hours on end. When they first arrived in Algeria, nearly six years before, they wondered how they would ever meet women, for they were hardly ever out of their houses. But God opened the way. Closed doors are no problem to God!

Desert Rain

March arrived at last and it was decided that Helen would go with Lilias on the missionary journey. And that's exactly what it was. They weren't tourists going to explore, and they certainly weren't holidaymakers going for a rest. This was a carefully planned expedition … but before they had gone very far their plans had to be changed.

Having travelled as far as Biskra, Lilias and Helen had to abandon all thought of camping, for the rain fell solidly and there were no stars to be seen. It seemed that God was telling them to visit the town of Touggourt.

'I know we'd decided to go round the villages,' Helen said. 'Do you think God really means us to go to a town instead?'

The two women prayed about it. When they prayed, they didn't just speak to God, they expected God to answer by showing them what they should do. And it certainly seemed that God was pointing them in the direction of Touggourt.'

'It's God's way that matters,' Helen said, 'not ours.' And Lilias completely agreed.

Before beginning their journey to Touggourt, Lilias did what she often did, she took out her small box of paints and her sketch pad and sat down on the little folding seat that she carried with her. Helen came to look at what her friend was going to paint.

'Isn't that amazing!' said Helen, 'and I didn't even notice it.'

'After rain the desert breaks into bloom almost immediately,' Lilias smiled. 'And I just love looking for the very first flowers. Their seeds lie there sleeping until the rain comes. Then, by the next day, there are tiny leaves and even tinier flowers in bloom. If we were to come back here tomorrow, there could be a yellow carpet of miniature flowers where a week ago there was only hot dry sand.'

Helen watched her friend paint. It always amazed her how Lilias could have just a few little blocks of paint in her box and from them mix whatever colour she wanted. The tiny leaves in the desert plant were a peculiar shade of green, quite unlike English grass green. With just a few touches on her blocks of paint Lilias had exactly the right colour on her brush.

'I don't know how she does that,' thought Helen. 'But I love watching.'

First Lilias painted the stems of the plant just in front of her seat, fine lines to guide the rest of the painting. Then she sketched in the leaves, each one different from the other. Helen watched, fascinated, as her friend dried her brush and then used it to lift some of the wet paint from the leaves to make parts of them lighter. And she was even more interested as Lilias touched the light red block of paint with the tip of her brush. Very carefully, while the leaves were still wet, the artist touched several of them and waited as the colour merged with the green and changed it.

'But the leaves aren't red,' Helen thought. Then, looking more closely at what was being painted, she saw that there was indeed a pink tinge to some of them. 'I would never have noticed that had Lilias not painted it in,' she decided.

As she watched Helen knew that, although she enjoyed drawing and painting, it was her friend who was the real artist. And she was right.

In the lid of her paint box Lilias mixed a tiny amount of the green she had made with a light yellow colour that reminded Helen of England and of primroses. Using exactly the same technique she'd used for the leaves, Lilias sketched tiny flower petals and then lifted some of the wet paint off with her dry brush. Then she used light red to paint the veins on the petals. As Helen watched, a little more green was applied to the stems to darken them. Lastly Lilias painted the jaggy thorns along each stem.

'It's interesting that so many desert plants have thorns,' commented Helen. 'But I think I understand why God made them like that. If they didn't have thorns, they'd be eaten as a tasty meal by whatever animals came along. And I guess after the seeds have waited so long in the baking desert heat they deserve to live longer than that.'

Lilias smiled at her friend. 'Beauty and thorns go together. For example, the Christian life is very beautiful. What could be more beautiful than living day by day knowing that Jesus is with us?' she asked. 'But there are thorns among the beauty: sad times, pain and suffering as well.'

'But think of the beauty after life here is over,' Helen pointed out. 'When we go to heaven there will be no pain or sadness, no sickness and no death.'

'That really will be beautiful,' agreed Lilias. 'And most beautiful of all will be seeing Jesus face to face! Imagine that.'

Helen was silent for what seemed a long time. 'I can't,' she decided. 'It's just too glorious even to begin to imagine.'

'And much too beautiful even to begin to paint,' said Lilias, washing her brushes and snapping her little paint box shut.

The painting done and her art things packed away, it was time for Lilias and Helen to set out on the journey to Touggourt. That meant four days spent in a horse-drawn trap. As they clip-clopped along the desert road, the women remembered their summer journeys to Europe in stagecoaches pulled by a team of horses.

'Do you remember the places we used to stay?' asked Helen, 'the spotless sheets and polished silver?'

Lilias did remember and the memory made her smile. 'I'm quite happy in an Algerian caravanserai. Are you?'

'I certainly am.'

The caravanserais, in which they stayed on the three nights of their journey, were small, rough rooms with no furniture. They were made especially for travellers who carried their bedding with them. Helen and Lilias were, by then, well-travelled and knew exactly what they needed. Each night, after unrolling their mats on their beds (canvas stretched over low bed frames), reading their Bibles and praying, they lay down and exhaustion sent them to sleep before the noises of the night had any chance of keeping them awake.

In her diary Lilias tells us about Touggourt.

'Touggourt was reached at last, and such a sunset over the desert! It is real desert here, the sand is fine and soft and deep. The streets are strange places, roofed in till they are twilight tunnels at the brightest and often quite dark for a bit in broad daylight. We got into a good many houses by the help of Abdullah, the guide who had come with us …'

Meet Abdullah. It was a strange thing for two women – especially two white women – to be travelling in the desert. For that reason alone they would have needed to pay a man to be with them, and that man was Abdullah. Travelling wasn't safe for a whole number of reasons, one of them being that there were bandits in the desert.

The two missionaries needed a guide to keep them safe in bandit territory. They also needed a guide because it would have been very easy for Lilias and Helen to get lost. Sand looks like sand whatever direction you look in. Sand hills, unlike ordinary hills, change their shapes. You can have a sand hill with pointed peaks one day and the next day the peaks will have blown flat and the same sand hill will have a rounded top. So Abdullah was needed because he knew the land and would take the women to where they wanted to go.

He was needed for another reason too. If two strange white women had arrived in a village on their own, they wouldn't have been welcomed into people's homes. With Abdullah to explain that they were harmless, and just wanted to tell them stories, they were sometimes invited in. Even when they were not, men and children would speak to them in the street. If they wanted to speak to women, they had to be invited into homes.

For a few days the missionaries worked in Touggourt, telling people about Jesus and handing out Christian booklets to the men they met. Nearly always they were taken eagerly. Often, the day after books were given out, men would wait for Lilias and Helen on the street to ask for other stories as they'd read the first ones overnight. Of course, the missionaries were always happy to give out another story about Jesus. The good thing about using books in missionary work was that they could be read over and over again, long after Lilias and Helen had moved on to another place.

A Mirage?

'We want to go to Oued Souf now,' Helen told Abdullah.

He thought they were crazy!

'Do you know what the journey will be like?' he asked.

'Yes,' Helen said. 'We know it's further into the desert and that there's no road.'

Abdullah shook his head. He was a guide, and he knew the way, but even he wasn't too keen. However, travel they did, on camels and with a mule to carry their luggage.

The journey was over eighty miles of cream-coloured sand with no road to show them the way and plenty of sand dunes for bandits to use as hiding places. Lilias and Helen prayed that God would keep them safe on their travels, and he did. As they rocked from side to side on their camels, the two women wondered what El Oued would be like. It was the main town in a little group of oasis villages. Lilias and Helen knew that it was most likely that nobody in El Oued would even have heard the name of Jesus before.

'Just imagine being the first to tell these people about Jesus,' Helen thought, as her camel trundled onwards.

Lilias was thinking exactly the same thing and, as mile followed slow sandy mile, the pair of them grew more and more excited. The missionaries knew that telling people that the Lord Jesus Christ is God's Son and our Saviour, is to tell them the best news in the whole wide world.

Two days after leaving Touggourt, Lilias saw something in the distance.

'Is it a mirage?' she wondered, for the sun was beating down on the sand and what she was seeing seemed to be moving before her eyes.

Abdullah pointed into the distance.

'That's El Oued,' said he. 'We're nearly there.'

'There's something very strange about the palm trees,' pointed out Helen, as they neared the town.

Lilias agreed. 'They must be a different kind in this part of Algeria. They are only about half the height of normal palms.'

'They are the same kind,' Abdullah told them. 'But it is so dry here they are planted much more deeply than usual. In fact, about half of the trunk of each palm tree is underground.'

'Half?' queried Helen.

Abdullah didn't like not being believed.

'Yes, half,' he said firmly. 'And they are planted that way so that their roots are as far down into the sand as possible. Then they reach the water a metre underground.

'Now I understand,' said Helen.

Abdullah looked a bit happier. He liked to show the European women that he knew much more about his country than they did. That was, of course, quite true! Feeling superior, he decided to take on the role of tour guide.

'You'll notice that many of the houses have domes rather than roofs and that the houses are also sunk into the sand to keep them out of the burning sun.'

To Helen and Lilias's surprise the houses were like beehives made of sand. In fact, they were called sand hives!

Abdullah explained that the sand was far too fine to be made into bricks and there were no stones to build with for hundreds of miles. When he said this, he waved his arms in every direction.

Lilias looked around them and there was nothing to be seen but sand, amazingly fine cream-coloured sand for as far as they could see in every direction.

Before they'd even reached the edge of the town the travellers were surrounded by children reaching out to touch their fair-coloured skin and to feel what European hair felt like. It was a bit like being attacked by curiosity.

'We have come with good news,' Lilias told the children.

But she could hardly be heard above the noise.

Abdullah was good at crowd control.

'These women have come from a faraway country,' he shouted. 'And they have come with good news about their God. They will tell you their stories tomorrow.'

No sooner had he shut his mouth than several of the older boys tried to lead the camels off in opposite directions, each with a different idea of where the strangers should go. Then some men joined the crowd but, as usual, there was hardly a woman to be seen.

'Why are you here?' several asked, all at once.

'What have you to do with us?' others wanted to know.

'Where do you come from?'

'Why have you come?'

Question after question after question came like gunfire. Helen and Lilias just waited quietly, for there was no point in speaking until the noise died down, at least a little bit.

By late afternoon some children had taken Lilias and Helen to meet their mothers. The women of Oued Souf were amazed that two Europeans could speak their language!

The people of Oued Souf were poor, but you would never have known it for they all wanted to feed the missionaries. Neither Helen nor Lilias had big appetites, in fact, they ate very small meals. So when they were given plate after plate of food they only took a little from each. As it was rude to leave food, they had to be very careful to hand the plates round the women so that an empty plate went back to the owner.

'Tomorrow we will go out in the street and meet the men,' Lilias said, before the two women lay down on their camp beds for the night.

'It's so strange,' answered Helen. 'The women of the town can't go out in the street among the men, but we can.'

'I know,' her friend agreed. 'And the men spend hours talking to us. Let's hope we sleep well first!'

The missionaries were absolutely right. Next day they were hardly in the street when the men started to gather. They had heard from their wives the stories Lilias had told them and they wanted to know more.

'Do you have any books that we can read for ourselves,' some men asked. 'We can read.'

Helen was carrying a bag full of Christian booklets and she handed one out to each of the men who said he could read.

'Can I have one?' an old man asked.

'He can't read,' said someone. 'Don't give him a book. That's a waste.'

The old man held on tightly to the book he'd been given. 'My son will read it to me,' he explained to Helen, who smiled and allowed him to keep it.

The men were out again looking for more books first thing the following morning.

'What I want you to do is this,' said Helen. 'I want you to swap books. When you've read the one we gave you, swap it with a friend who has a different one. Then by the end of the week you'll all have read all the books.'

'And my son will have read all of them to me too,' the old man told Helen. 'That was a good story he read to me last night. It was about the God Jesus feeding 5,000 men out of just a few bread rolls and some small fish.'

He was holding the book in his hand.

'Would anyone swap this book for another one?' he asked. Someone did and the old man was pleased to have another book for his son to read to him.

Mahfoud, Dahman and Mohammed

Helen and Lilias were away from Algiers for nearly two months on that trip. While they were travelling, the work in the city was led by the other missionaries. That became the pattern for the years that were to follow. Lilias and one of her friends, usually Helen or Blanche, went on missionary journeys lasting months at a time while the others worked with the Arab people in Algiers.

'This is a wonderful day,' Blanche said, not long after Lilias and Helen returned. 'Imagine us having an Arab prayer meeting! We've prayed for them for years, now some of them are coming here to pray for their own people.'

After the meeting the women talked over a cup of tea.

'I believe God will answer our prayers,' said Blanche. 'Nearly everyone prayed for more Arab men to come to our meetings and I believe that God will bring them.'

The other women agreed that God was well able to do that. The very next day eight Arab men came, none of them ever having been to a Christian meeting before!

That night there was another prayer meeting with only the missionaries present and their prayers were all saying thank-you to God!

The next day three Arab boys, who had become Christians, arrived at the door.

'Come in Mahfoud, Dahman and Mohammed,' said Helen.

The boys came in and were given syrup sandwiches (their favourite!) and a drink of tea.

'Can we have some books?' they asked.

Helen smiled. 'Of course. But I thought you'd read all the books we have in Arabic.'

'We have,' agreed Mahfoud. 'But we want to give them to people who've never heard about Jesus.'

Helen sat down beside the boys. 'Tell me what you're thinking about,' she said.

Mahfoud was their spokesman. 'We've seen you going from door to door along the streets,' he explained. 'And we've seen you giving books to people who can read. We'd like to do that too.'

Helen was thrilled, but a little concerned.

'Do you realise that people might not welcome you at their doors?' she asked. 'They might be polite to a European visitor, but not be very polite to you.'

'We know that,' said Dahman. 'But we want to do what Jesus wants us to do.'

Helen looked out some gospels and gave them to the boys.

'We'll be praying for you,' she told them, as they went out into the street. 'And be careful.'

Not only boys had become Christians, there was a little group of men too. They met with the missionaries to study the Bible and pray. And there were also some families. One woman, her name was Taitum, made the little church grow in size quite regularly because she kept having babies!

Lilias Trotter was a real adventurer. It was as if she could picture faraway places where no Christian had ever been and hear faraway people who had never heard of Jesus calling out to her. So it was no surprise when, early in 1895, she and Blanche were packing up for another journey, the longest and hardest they had ever done.

When you think of Lilias and her fellow missionaries believing that God wanted them to tell the people of Algeria about Jesus, it would be helpful to remember some facts and figures. At that time Algeria was the second biggest country in Africa.

The U.K. is 94,251 square miles and the U.S.A. is 3,679,191 square miles. Algeria was then 9.5 times bigger than the U.K., and almost a quarter of the size of the U.S.A.! The borders of Algeria have changed since then. Remember that as you read more of Lilias and Blanche's travels.

'Now, what all do we need?' asked Blanche, as they prepared for their trip to the southeast of Algeria towards Tunisia.

Lilias reeled off a list.

'We need the tent, our camp beds and our cooking things.'

Blanche laughed. 'I'm not going to forget them! But what needs to be packed in the goatskins?'

The women didn't use suitcases, they would have been very awkward when carried by a mule. Instead they wrapped their clothes and books in coloured goatskins which could be tied in bundles and strapped to their mule.

They carried as few clothes as possible and as many Gospels as they could. Of course, Lilias's watercolour paints and sketchbook always went with her.

'Where are you going this time?' asked Taitum, who was sitting in the kitchen at Rue du Croissant surrounded by her children.

Lilias explained that they planned to travel for several months. 'We'll go by train first and then by trap. After that we'll mount our camels and head to the south, through the desert and over the mountains, till we reach two big towns called Nefta and Tozeur.'

'They don't sound Algerian,' commented Taitum.

Lilias smiled. 'You're quite right,' she said. 'They are in Tunisia, just over the Algerian border.'

Taitum looked worried. 'Will you be safe?'

The missionary explained that God would be with them wherever they went. She then told Taitum that they hoped to come back by Oued Souf and Touggourt, where they had been before, to see the people there. After that their plan was to investigate other places that they might go to in the future.'

'How long will you be away?' Taitum wanted to know.

Lilias suggested that it might be as long as four or five months.

Taitum patted her tummy and smiled. 'There will be another new baby here by the time you get back.'

Lilias painted a lovely picture when she and Blanche were on that long adventure. It showed a farmer sowing seed. And, in a way, that's exactly what they were doing. They were telling men and women, boys and girls about the Lord Jesus Christ. And they were praying that little seeds of belief would grow in their hearts and minds and that they would become Christians. Sometimes that happened right away, but other times the little seeds took years to grow.

Lilias's Journal

As they travelled Lilias kept a journal (a kind of diary illustrated with her own paintings) and it was 186 pages long! Lilias and Blanche were accompanied by Abdullah and two camel drivers. Their names were Keroui and Aoun. There were also three camels, a mule and a donkey. That made quite a little caravan of animals and people. And that's not a modern kind of caravan in which you might have a holiday! It is a row of animals and people walking through the desert, often in a straight line one in front of another.

The 186 page journal gives you an idea of how long their travels were. In fact, just as Lilias had said, they were away for a whole five months. They crossed mountain ranges and visited strings of villages as they did so. And, of course, they trekked over hundreds of miles of desert. In her journal Lilias describes one desert journey which was a bit different, and not different in a good way!

We trekked on 'through a blinding blizzard of sand. ... Every trace of footprints was swept away, and the track was invisible as we journeyed on, to our eyes at any rate. A knotted head of broom (a kind of bush) now and then proved that the men knew what they were about and that we were keeping right.'

'Towards evening the gusts lessened, and the stars came out of the brown sand-clouds. The next morning dawned clear and calm showing, on the western half of the horizon, range after range of snow-like sand-hills, rose-tinted in the sunrise. And we knew that buried among them were the villages for which we were making ...'

One of the problems about amazing sand-storms like that was how much they changed the countryside. Thousands of tons of sand could be blown about; so many tons that hills that used to be to the left of the track were blown to the right. And a village you could see in the far distance could be seen no more, for it was covered in sand. Of course, bushes that Abdullah knew, and that showed him where to go, could be blown 20 miles away.

The following day, after they had done another day's travelling, Lilias and Blanche settled down in their tent once again..

'Abdullah can be so bad-tempered and difficult,' said Lilias. 'And sometimes it looks as if he doesn't know his way around the desert-lands at all. But ...'

Blanche finished her sentence.

'I know what you're going to say,' she smiled. 'The sandstorm made everything look so different yet we're still on the right track. Abdullah does know where he's going after all.'

Lilias pulled her blanket up over herself and settled down on her low hammock bed for the night.

'Just remind me of that next time Abdullah loses his temper, waves his arms in every direction, and tells us what fools we are!'

Before they fell asleep, both women had the same thought. Perhaps if they were responsible for taking two odd strangers across a desert that kept changing what it looked like, they might get cross sometimes too.

Five months after leaving Algiers, Blanche and Lilias arrived back. Imagine how much they were looking forward to seeing their friends again! Some good things had happened and Helen told Lilias and Blanche all about them. But they knew right away that there was something troubling their friends in Rue du Croissant.

'I'm afraid things are not good with us,' Francis Brading told Blanche and Lilias, when the excitement of their arrival was over. 'You know that the climate in Algiers has never really been good for our children,' he went on.

Blanche nodded.

'Well,' said Francis, 'while you were away they took ill again, dangerously ill. The doctor has told us that their lives are in danger if we stay here.'

There was a silence while Lilias and Blanche took in what was being said.

'Francis isn't well either,' said Reba, his wife. 'The doctor says that the climate is making him ill too.'

There was no way around it; the Bradings would have to go home to England. How sad Helen, Blanche and Lilias were to say their goodbyes. And the truth is that, although Francis and Reba were relieved to be going to a climate that would be better for them all, they were also sad to be leaving. It was a time of change in the mission work based in Rue du Croissant.

The Brading family were not the only ones that the climate in Algeria affected. Lilias, Blanche and Helen also suffered from the heat. Most years they left the country for a month or two. They would then visit the U.K. or different parts of Europe. Shortly after Francis, Reba and their children left the mission, Lilias headed off to England for a few months and ended up staying from July 1895 to January 1896. She was utterly exhausted.

'You're meant to be resting,' a friend told her, when she found Lilias sitting writing on sheet after sheet of paper.

The missionary smiled. 'This is restful,' she said.

'May I ask what it is?'

'I'm writing a book,' admitted Lilias. 'I think it will be called "Parables of the Cross", and that tells you what it's about.'

Pointing to a painting that was still drying, her friend asked if the picture was for the book.

'Yes,' replied Lilias. 'I've almost finished the paintings I'm going to use in it. I've done fifteen and I think I need one more. Would you like to see them?'

The other woman was delighted to be asked. Lilias gave her a folder of watercolour paintings and continued with her writing.

There was absolute silence for almost an hour before her friend spoke again.

'These are absolutely lovely,' she said. 'My favourite is the dandelion seed-head.'

It showed a dandelion clock – that's the fluffy seed-head that's left after all the yellow petals have withered and dropped. To the right of it Lilias had painted seven tiny seeds being blown away in the wind. And round the seed-head were the words, 'I am now ready to be offered.'

Lilias explained that the dandelion had to let its petals die before the seeds could develop. And then it had to let all the seeds blow away before any new plants could grow.

'You see,' said Lilias, 'the dandelion has to give itself away completely for God to create new plants. And those who follow Jesus have to give all they are and all they have for him to use.'

'That will make a lovely book,' her friend told Lilias. And it did.

Children Everywhere!

Not long after Lilias returned to Algiers two more English women came to join the team. They were Gertrude Targgot and May Eustace.

'Look at all these children,' said Gertrude, as she went out the great studded door of 2 Rue du Croissant. 'They are everywhere. If you look to the right, they bump into your left side. And if you look to your left, they'll crash into you on the right side.'

May grinned. 'There's certainly no shortage of children in the streets, steps and lanes around our house.'

When the women discussed this at their next meal, Lilias had an idea.

'Do you think we could run classes for some of the children?' she asked.

It was decided to begin by running a class for boys. They prayed about it and then the class began. At first it went well. But then the boys started playing up, just in little ways at first and then they started to behave really badly, so badly that the class had to be stopped.

'What about a class for girls?' asked May. 'They might listen better.'

Gertrude wondered if they might try a class for Jewish girls. There was a good number of Jewish families in an area of new houses very near to where the missionaries lived. And that worked. The Jewish girls loved the class and they listened very eagerly to what they heard about Jesus.

'The only day that women go out is Friday,' May said, when they were wondering how best to meet the Arab women. 'That's the day the women and girls go to the cemeteries.'

Gertrude looked a little puzzled. 'I find that very strange,' she admitted. 'They are in their houses all week and on Fridays, when the men and boys are all at the mosques, they choose to go to cemeteries.'

Lilias explained that the women gathered in cemeteries to meet up with their friends. That was the only place they were allowed to meet. And the men were quite happy for them to go there because they took flowers to put on the graves of their ancestors.

That sparked an idea and, before long, Lilias and the other missionaries rented a room near the cemetery where Arab women could go for a cup of tea and a chat after their weekly trip to lay down flowers. Of course, they told their visitors about the Lord Jesus, and how he rose from the dead on the first Easter Sunday.

'We've never heard of anyone rising from the dead!' an Arab woman said, after a chat with Lilias. 'Tell us who that was and how it happened?'

Lilias was very happy to do that. She loved talking to the women about the Lord Jesus. There was nothing that she liked better.

From that time on more and more people became interested in God, and the little church in Algiers grew. Some people went for a short while and then stopped, but a good number kept going. One of them was Belaid, who had become a Christian when he was in England.

'How did you learn about Jesus before you started coming here to church?' Blanche asked.

'I had my Bible,' explained the man. 'I just read my Bible over and over again. That's how I got to know Jesus better.'

Of course, coming to meetings and being with other Christians also helped Belaid.

The house in Rue du Croissant was often full of noise and laughter because children were welcome. When they knocked on the heavy studded door they were asked in and often treated to syrup sandwiches. Two little girls were especially welcome. Their names (nicknames really) were Pink Shell and Brown Berry.

'The girls were just street urchins,' Lilias explained, in a letter to a friend. 'They had nowhere to call home and looked to kind people in the city to feed them. Slowly the two girls wormed their way into our hearts. And it was Blanche who gave in and eventually adopted them as her own.'

Of course, Lilias did many sketches of the two little girls and it was quite obvious from her journal that Blanche wasn't the only one who loved Pink Shell and Brown Berry. While they still missed the Brading children, now Blanche had two little girls of her own and they lived as a happy family in that very big house. What Lilias thought about 2 Rue du Croissant the first time she saw it, turned out to be absolutely true. It was a splendid house for playing hide and seek!

Over the years there was a great deal of coming and going between Algeria and Britain. Some people went to help the missionaries for short times and others spent longer with them. Lilias, Blanche and Helen also came and went because most years they all needed to get away from the heat for a time. The climate in Algiers sapped their strength and energy. It was especially hard on Lilias who had a heart condition and – despite all you've read about her – she tired easily. Although she loved travelling, and was a real adventurer, it was hard work.

In the spring of 1900 Helen and Lilias went south to the desert town of Tolga. There they rented a house.

'It's strange not to be staying in our tent,' commented Lilias, as they investigated the little house they would live in for some weeks.

'I like it,' Helen said.

Later she wrote to a friend.

'The walls are made of earth and the floor too. Thatched palm leaves are on the low roof. I don't imagine they would keep out the rain but that's not a problem in the desert. There's a little courtyard and that's where we will sleep, outside under the stars.'

When the two missionaries discussed what they would do in Tolga, they decided to pitch their tent in the courtyard and hold their meetings there. They were glad they did for people came, and then more people came ... and then even more people came! Most of them were men, as usual, and some were very keen to hear about Jesus. It made Lilias want to come back to Tolga to stay, at least for a longer time than the three weeks they planned to be there. I've no doubt that was what she and Helen talked about on the long journey back to Algiers.

The Map-maker

On her next missionary trip Lilias showed how well organised she was. They were in the small town of Blida, once again renting rooms rather than camping.

'What are you writing?' asked an Arab man, who wanted to talk to her.

Lilias looked up from her sheet of paper and smiled. She wondered how she would explain what she was doing.

'Back in England,' she began, 'every road has a name and every house has a number.'

'Why?' asked the man, who was very puzzled at the idea.

Lilias said that towns were much bigger there and names and numbers made it easier to find where you were going. The man grinned.

'I've drawn a plan of Blida and the villages round about. See, here is the road up the hill.' Lilias pointed to a straight road on the map she was drawing.

The man looked at it, thought for a minute, and then pointed to his house which was on that road. He was very pleased with himself!

Lilias explained that she was giving all the streets and lanes names and all the houses numbers.

'Do you think thousands of people are going to come to live in Blida?' laughed the man, very amused at the thought.

Lilias laughed too. 'No,' she said. 'But using a map like this means that we can visit every home and then make a mark on the paper to show we've been there. While we are here this time we will visit some homes and, when we come back, we'll visit others.'

'Will you visit my home?' he asked.

'I hope we will,' the missionary said. 'We want to tell everyone about Jesus and not miss anyone out.'

Back in Algiers the usual work went on and new work started.

'We have a plan we would like to discuss with you,' Lilias told Madam Gayral, a local shopkeeper.

The woman ran an embroidery store. Threads and fabrics were sold there for those who wanted to do their own sewing. And finished embroidery was sold there too, especially the beautiful stitchery for which Algeria was famous.

'Would you come to our home in Rue du Croissant and teach young girls how to do traditional embroidery?' Madam Gayral was asked.

Lilias explained that she hoped young wives – sometimes as young as twelve – would come to their classes.

'That's the perfect age for them to learn,' said the shopkeeper-cum-embroiderer.

An arrangement was made for Madam Gayral to teach the girls and then sell their embroideries. That worked very well indeed, and some of the girls even stayed after the class to learn to read.

'Hardly any women can read,' said a young wife, who had just passed her thirteenth birthday. 'We are very special.'

Lilias sat down beside the little group of girls and explained that they were indeed very special, so special that Jesus died on the cross so that they could have their sins forgiven and go to heaven one day.

Life was not easy for English missionaries in Algeria at that time. The government often delayed their work, or even stopped what they were doing. It was much less complicated for French people who were supported by the government. That's why it was especially good when some French missionaries came to join the team. They were Paul and Philomene Villon and Michel Olives. French people had much greater freedom in Algeria than the English did, and men had much more freedom than women.

Lilias and her friends had prayed for God to bring men to the mission team and they were delighted with the new arrivals. It wasn't long before plans were being made for them. Sitting in Rue du Croissant they discussed the possibilities.

'The government and the leaders of the mosque say that we should not try to make people become Christians,' Helen said. 'But that doesn't stop us being friends with them.'

Everyone agreed.

'And it doesn't stop them coming to us for coffee,' added Paul.

Lilias shook her head. 'I'm afraid it does,' she told him. 'The Arab people have been banned from coming into our house.'

Paul explained that wasn't what he was thinking.

'Do you see that little café across the road?' he asked, pointing out the window. 'We could make that into a meeting room where men could come freely. They'd be able to relax over their coffee and talk about the Bible at the same time.'

The other missionaries immediately realised that was a splendid idea, and before long the gospel café was up and running.

When Lilias went off to Europe for her summer break that year she felt different from the years before. Until then the work in the city of Algiers stopped most summers as the missionaries all went away to recover from the heat. Now there were enough of them for the work to go on all year round. That felt good and she thanked God for it.

Hard Times

It was December 1901 and the two friends, Lilias and Blanche were back in Tolga. At first things seemed to be going well. They settled into a local house and people came to see them and to talk. Not only that, strangers travelling through Tolga heard about Jesus and then went on their journeys still talking about him.

'They are missionaries without even knowing it!' Blanche said. 'When they meet strangers on the road, and stop to talk to them, they'll tell them the stories of Jesus that they heard from us.'

'We'll pray that will happen,' agreed Lilias.

And they did.

Just as things were going smoothly the women heard some bad news. A government official had been told about their mission work and was coming to see what they were doing. He came, he was very polite … and then he told them, once again, to stop trying to make people Christians. Of course, nobody can make someone a Christian except God alone, but the government official didn't understand that.

Blanche and Lilias felt sad.

'Things were going so well,' said Blanche. 'This is just heartbreaking.'

'But God doesn't make mistakes,' Lilias pointed out. 'He must want us somewhere else.'

That happened in 1902, and for the next while things just became harder and harder. They had to be so very careful not to upset the officials and not to break the law. By the next year the children's groups they ran in Algiers had gone down from 100 to only a handful of children. Some people even went to court and told lies about the missionaries to get them into trouble. There seemed to be no end to the hard things they had to face.

When Lilias went back to England in the summer of 1903 it seemed as if the work in Algeria was slowing down to a stop. But it was while she was away from her beloved Arab people that a little chink of light sent from God began to shine through the darkness.

'Although people can no longer come to Rue du Croissant, and often we can't go to them, they can still read,' she thought. Then, lying back on her pillow, for she was quite ill that summer, she remembered how many girls and women had been taught to read while they'd been doing embroidery in their home. 'I wonder ....'

As she lay there, her heart weak and her energy very low, Lilias's mind had time to think through a new idea. She talked it over with a friend.

'In the Bible we read that Jesus taught people by telling stories that they could easily understand.'

'You mean parables like the Good Samaritan and the Lost Sheep,' her friend replied.

'Yes,' agreed Lilias. 'I've been wondering if we could write stories set in an Algerian background that would teach people about Jesus. They could be written in the beautiful Arabic script, not educated Arabic, but the language the people speak in their own homes.'

Her friend nodded. 'And would you illustrate them with your paintings of Algerian scenes and people?'

Lilias's face shone. The idea was coming together very quickly now that it had been spoken aloud.

'We could do one story a month and then people would begin to look forward to them and collect them.'

'And pass them round their friends,' suggested her companion.

So it was that during her months at home, when Lilias's heart was weak and her health poor, the missionary's brain, pencil and paintbrush were busy writing stories and drawing and painting illustrations to go along with them. On her return to Algeria, plans were made to begin this new work. Before long the booklets, beautifully written, copied carefully and bound together with ribbon, were being handed out to people who would not hear about Jesus any other way.

Arabic writing, unlike English, is very curvy and artistic. The mix of graceful Arabic writing and Lilias's lovely paintings was quite beautiful.

'The people love beauty,' Helen said, as she held one of the stories called 'The Debt of Ali Ben Omar' in her hands.

'They look so different from British books,' Lilias commented. 'Much softer, somehow.'

'I think that's because we've used the traditional cream paper. Its rough texture makes your watercolour paintings look as if they are on canvas!'

Lilias looked at the painting she was working on. It was of an Arab woman and child. For a few minutes she allowed herself to think back over the years to John Ruskin trying to persuade her to become a full-time artist, to be principal of a school of art for women in London.

'Would I have been happier doing that rather than going through all the troubles with the Algerian government?' she asked herself.

'No!'

She knew that she was where God wanted her to be and that she was at her happiest telling people about Jesus.

Then she smiled. 'Perhaps,' she thought, 'I'm at my happiest on the back of a camel in the remotest parts of the Algerian desert!'

What Lilias and Helen could never have imagined was that over the years to come many of these parable books would be translated into other languages and used in different countries. God doesn't waste anything!

Although Lilias Trotter was able to paint and write, she wasn't at all well.

'You need a very long rest,' her doctor said. 'Six months, at least.'

Helen, Blanche and the others were dismayed.

'She'll never rest for anything like that length of time,' they decided.

But Lilias's body was agreeing with her doctor. She knew she was completely exhausted. For months the missionary spent most of her time in her little room in

Rue du Croissant with some of her Arab friends looking after her as well as the missionaries. Being in her room didn't dull her interest in what was going on, however.

'We're just getting ready to go,' Paul and Michel said, when they visited Lilias in her room before leaving for her beloved Tolga.

'I'll be with you in prayer,' she told them, and then tapped a large folded sheet of paper that was lying on her bed. 'And I'll be following your every step on this.'

'What is it?' Michel asked.

Lilias opened up the sheet and spread it over the bed. It's a map I drew of Tolga and the villages round about it. I'll be thinking about you as you go to this home and that one,' she said, pointing to the houses where people she remembered lived. 'And you'll need this with you so that you can take note of your door-to-door visiting.'

Taking a second sheet from underneath the first one, Lilias gave the two men a copy of her map to use on their travels. Because Lilias wrote a journal, we know that she did follow the work that Paul and Michel did because she wrote down what she was thinking of and who she was praying for.

Dar Naama

Part of the reason the missionaries found the summer heat unbearable was that they wore English clothes that were not best suited to the climate, but partly because it was just roasting hot.

'Wouldn't it be wonderful if we could have a little place outside the city where we could go to rest, just for a week or so at a time,' Blanche said.

She didn't only say that to her missionary friends, she also talked about it with God, asking him to show her if there was such a place to be had. God heard her prayers and gave Blanche a lovely surprise. He provided them with a ramshackle old house surrounded by shady trees that kept the house cool in the summer heat. There was a vineyard there too and a pine wood where she could sit out in the air but not in the sun. It was perfect. Of course it was, God doesn't make mistakes!

'We've called the house Dar Naama,' Blanche told a visitor, soon after the house was bought. 'That means House of Grace.'

'What a lovely name for a lovely place,' her visitor said. 'And it is so cool here compared to the city! You'll all be able to relax here, especially because it's so close. You won't have a tiring journey to get here.'

Lilias, who needed to travel less and rest more, found wonderful things to paint at Dar Naama. The parable books needed illustrations and this was the perfect place for her to paint them.

'I have always loved the smell of pine wood,' she told Blanche, as she sat in the shade of the pines sketching. 'In fact, over the years I've sometimes dreamed about resting in a pine wood. Now God has been good and given us one to enjoy.'

'There are not only shady pines,' Blanche said. 'God has also given us trees for fruit. There are cherries, pears, figs, walnuts and oranges too. And nettles.'

Lilias had already noticed the nettles! And she'd noticed the orange trees too as her friend discovered when she looked at that day's painting. Lilias had done a lovely watercolour of an orange tree with its oranges, still green, waiting to ripen.

About this time Lilias's journal began to change a little bit. Not all of the illustrations were paintings as she now had a box camera. With her artist's eye, she took very good black and white photographs. From them we can see what the missionaries looked like in their long skirts, fitted jackets and large hats. The Arab people must have been so much cooler and more comfortable in their simple loose flowing clothes.

In some countries missionaries decided to wear the same clothes as the locals, but that was something that Lilias and her colleagues never did. Dressed as they were, they would certainly have been noticed as they walked through the city of Algiers, and even more so as they travelled into new parts of the desert lands that they'd never visited before. No wonder news of their coming reached towns and villages before they did!

The missionaries sat talking in an upper room in Rue du Croissant.

'Is it my imagination,' asked Helen, 'or do you think the government is being less hard on us just now?'

'It's strange that you should say that,' one of the others replied. 'I met an official in a lane the other day. Usually he scowls at me and tells me to watch out and that we should be minding our own business. That day he just said, "Good morning" and walked on by. I don't mean that he was friendly, but he was certainly not unfriendly.'

'That's interesting,' said Lilias. 'We must pray about it.'

As the weeks of 1906 passed and became months it was clear that things were changing.

'God has heard our prayers and answered them,' smiled Lilias.

Arab people once again started speaking to them in the street and even coming to the door of their home in Rue du Croissant.

'Do you think the time has come to start up some of our classes and clubs again?'

They wondered if it was too early to do that and decided it was not. So serious planning began and things happened quickly.

'The women and girls are so glad to be back at their embroidery classes again.' Helen said. 'They've missed them so much.'

Lilias agreed. 'They even asked if we could tell them Bible stories while they are sewing.'

'And there are more boys than ever coming to learn woodwork,' said another missionary. 'Some of them are really good. I hope they'll get jobs as carpenters when they grow up.'

'We are even training some artists,' Lilias laughed delightedly. Being an artist herself she loved seeing other artists work.

Helen was puzzled. 'What do you mean?' she asked.

Lilias smiled. 'I mean the brushwork class we're running for younger boys. If you look at the writing they do with their brushes, it is just as lovely as a painting. Arabic script, written as they write it, is a thing of beauty.'

Everyone agreed.

Those were not the only things that were able to start up again. The Algiers Mission Band, as the group was then called, was even able to open up the room in Rue du Croissant that had been a mosque and use it for Sunday services.

'Of course,' wrote Lilias, in a letter to a friend, 'we have had to rig up a screen down the middle of the room to keep men and women apart. They never worship together in Arab culture.'

The café opened once more and men gathered there in the evenings after work to talk, and much of the talk was about Jesus.

So it was that, after some years of opposition from the government, the anti-British feeling grew less and the work of mission was able to go on openly. The truth is that it never really stopped, but it was much, much better.

Now, just when they were needed, God began to call more people to be missionaries in Algeria. In fact, five new workers went out in 1907, the most that had ever gone out in a year. Not only that, but travelling changed too when some of the workers started going around on bicycles for local journeys. The bicycles were carried as part of their luggage on long trips and then used to get between the scattered villages.

Lilias, who was by then fifty-four years old, still loved the desert. That September she and Annie Whistler (one of the new missionaries) spent some weeks at Bou Saada, which was between Algiers and Tolga. While they were there, Lilias wrote and painted even more than usual, as well as going from door to door to speak with people about Jesus.

Another thing which took a great deal of time was a project to translate the Gospel of Luke into ordinary Arabic. The Gospel of Luke is the third book of the New Testament and it tells the life story of Jesus.

'Why is this so important?' someone asked Lilias, one day.

She looked up from her pile of papers and thought for a minute before answering.

'Languages are strange,' she said. 'Sometimes we speak very politely as if we were speaking to grand strangers. But when we are with our families we speak differently. For example, it's the difference between saying "Mother" and "Mama", or the difference between "Excuse me, would you be agreeable to me joining you for coffee?" and "Would you like to come for a coffee?"

'There already is a translation of Luke's Gospel but it is in what I would call grand language. We are trying to tell the same story in ordinary Arabic, the kind of language women use when they are talking to one another, or children use when they speak to their dads. Does that make sense?'

'It makes very good sense,' was the answer. 'I think that grand language, as you call it, speaks to our heads and ordinary language speaks to our hearts.'

Lilias smiled warmly. 'That's exactly what I was trying to say! But,' she added, 'it is really hard work finding just the right words to speak to people's hearts.'

It was Christmas Eve 1908 when a special parcel arrived at Rue du Croissant. Inside were the very first copies of the newly-printed copies of Luke's Gospel.

That evening Lilias wrote in her journal, 'So the first Gospel that will be understood from cover to cover by the Arabs of Algeria goes out on a floodtide of hope in the same Lord over all …'

Lilias had travelled to England a few months before that, and to Sweden and Germany too. People in all these counties, and in many others besides, had heard about the work being done in the city of Algiers and the country of Algeria and had been praying for it. When the parcel full of Gospels in ordinary Arabic arrived that Christmas Eve it was in answer to all their prayers. Lilias and her friends called it 'God's Christmas present' and I've no doubt that it was the best Christmas they had ever had.

Digging for Water

Helen and Lilias sat side by side on the train as it wound its way along the mountainside towards Oran, in the western province of Algeria. They were heading for the town of Relizane.

'This is a new beginning,' said Helen, as she looked out the window at clumps of prickly pear bushes.

These usually surrounded houses and sometimes, as the train chugged along, the only way they knew they were passing villages was by the prickly pears.

'It is indeed,' agreed Lilias, 'and quite a change for all of us.'

'I'm really looking forward to working in Relizane,' Helen told her friend, 'though it will be very different from Algiers.'

'And you won't mind living and working alone there?' her friend asked.

'No,' said Helen. 'I don't think I will. And our missionary friends will come and go. But I must admit I'm glad that Philomene is staying with me for a little while to start with.'

Following the long journey, the two women had some interesting work to do. They had to find furniture for the little house that Helen was going to be staying in. It was just like the ones on either side of it. There was nothing to show that it was a mission house or that the women who stayed there were not ordinary Arab villagers.

'These are exactly what I want for a table and for storing things,' Helen said, as they looked around a jenny-all-things shop.

Do you know what a jenny-all-things shop is? It's the kind of shop that has everything, including all kinds of interesting second-hand things you'd not find elsewhere, and that most people would call junk.

Helen was pointing to some old wooden crates.

'And that pile of boxes over there could be used for storing our parable books,' she went on.

Most Europeans would have looked round and seen what they thought was rubbish. But Helen and Lilias viewed with different eyes, because by then they looked at things as an Arab villager would. They were keen recyclers before modern-day recycling had been invented!

Shortly after the house was furnished, and Helen and her guests had settled in, it was time for Lilias to move on. Before leaving the three women talked about the work that would be done in Relizane. With the help of a local French minister Helen would start door-to-door visiting and then try to begin the kind of classes and groups that she knew so well from Rue du Croissant. It was indeed a new beginning.

Blanche was already at another town called Miliana and Lilias joined her there.

'So we are house-hunting today,' Blanche said, the day after her friend arrived.

When you think of house-hunting, you perhaps think of the number of rooms you would like, the number of bathrooms, what kind of garden would be good to relax in and how near you would be to your school. Lilias and Blanche had other ideas. They were looking for the kind of house their Arab neighbours would be living in. By then missionaries knew that the best way to get to know village people was to live just as they did, in the same kind of very simple houses.

After Miliana, Lilias was on her travels again, this time to Blida. Michel Olives and his wife were working there now. They were already living in a traditional cottage. When we want a drink of water, we turn on a tap. When the missionaries needed water, they had to draw it from a well and there was a hitch with the well at Blida, a big hitch. There was no water in it!

'We've dug down more than 150 feet,' Michel told Lilias, 'and it's still dry at the bottom.'

'That's a problem,' said Lilias.

'It's actually a problem in more ways than one,' replied Michel. 'It's a problem because we don't have our own source of water. But it's also a problem because the villagers are saying that if our God means us to be here, it's strange that he's not giving us water.'

Lilias looked thoughtful. 'I can see what they mean,' she smiled. 'Do we believe that God wants us to be here?'

Michel and his wife were sure that he did.

'Then,' said Lilias, 'I think we should keep on digging.'

So the digging of the well continued. Of course, it was very dark all that way down and nobody could see what was at the bottom. At the end of one day's work they dropped a heavy stone and waited to hear what would happen. There was a dull thud.

'There's no water there at all,' an Arab villager said. 'I think your God wants you to go away from here.'

The next day was the same, and the next. But the following day, when the stone reached the bottom, there was a splash!

'Water!' shouted everyone, even the Arab villager who was back to see what was going on.

There was a moment's silence and then the missionaries all began to sing, 'Praise God from whom all blessings flow!'

And the blessing that flowed that day was water!

So it was that after some years when the work in Algeria was really hard going because of the government, now in 1909 so much was happening all at once. Amazingly, nine new people came out to be missionaries with the Algiers Mission Band. That gave them a total of 20 workers. There was plenty of work to do and it seemed that there was even freedom to do it.

'What are you thinking?' asked one of the workers.

Lilias, who had been sitting painting a beautiful flower, was lost in thought. She didn't even hear the question.

'What are you thinking?'

Lilias looked up. 'I started off thinking that God was so good for making this beautiful flower. Then I thanked him that he was so good for allowing us to live and work in Algeria. And I just kept finding more and more reasons for thanking him. God is SO good.'

New things always seemed to be starting up. Lilias and those who worked with her were never short of ideas. One thing that worked well was a spring conference which was held at Dar Naama. That was where all the missionaries met together to learn and to pray, to talk things through and to enjoy each other's company.

More Arab-style homes were bought as bases for even more missionaries. Ten new members joined the team in 1911 and 1912. New missionaries meant more work could be done. So children's camps were started and a work among blind men.

The work missionaries do is serious – they go to tell people that they are sinners and they need the one and only saviour, Jesus Christ. But that doesn't mean that they are boring old people who disapprove of laughing. Here's what Lilias wrote in her diary after one particularly fun evening.

'We had what the Americans would call a surprise party tonight. I came down to supper and found the whole of the younger generation in local costumes made of the bedcovers and curtains of their rooms …, with their tablecloths draped round their heads!'

The surprise party was to celebrate New Year. And the 'younger generation' was some young women who had gone to Algiers for just a few months to help those who were there full-time.

'It's lovely to feel the cool breeze,' said Blanche, relaxing on the deck of a steamer as it sailed out of the harbour. 'The heat in the city in July is hard to bear.'

Blanche, Helen, Lilias and four others from the Algiers Mission Band were on their way to a Sunday School Convention to be held in Switzerland. While there was time to relax on the steamer, Lilias also made time to work.

'Blanche,' she said to her friend, 'would you mind listening to some of my ideas?'

Smiling, Blanche thought to herself that she'd spent years listening to Lilias's ideas!

'I've been trying to work out the different ways we have of telling the Arab people about Jesus and this is what I've come up with.

1. The Christian café.
2. Using a Christian storyteller. Some verses of the Bible have already been written in a kind of rhyming style that makes them easier to learn and we could do more of that.
3. A place where women could go to be quiet and apart. The only places they go just now are cemeteries.
4. More embroidery groups for girls. Their fathers don't mind them coming to do embroidery because we do traditional Algerian work. Of course, they learn about Jesus while there are sewing.

And

5. We could run a guest house for families.

Even when travelling abroad to a conference, Lilias Trotter's mind was working on what could be done when they got back!

Growing Old

As time went on, Lilias spent more of the year in Rue du Croissant working as leader of the Algiers Mission Band. There was so much organising to do.

'When I go home to heaven,' she told a friend once, 'I'll be happy not to be organising things.'

Each year she did a tour of the various mission stations, by train, carriage, camel and, eventually by van – and what a van!

'This van could have been made just for us,' Lilias commented to Blanche. 'All its odd little spaces are prefect for books, leaflets and everything else we carry with us. We couldn't have found anything better.'

Blanche laughed. 'It's certainly different from anything else on the road.'

It was. It had been built for a lion tamer and his lion!

Blanche and Lilias were old friends. They had arrived together in Algiers in 1888 and now, twenty-seven years later, they were leaving together to go to Cairo in Egypt for three months.

'Enjoy your holiday,' one of their Arab friends said, as they waved goodbye.

Blanche smiled. 'I don't think there's going to be much time for holiday,' she thought, and she was right.

When they were settled in the flat that was to be their Cairo home, the two women went through the case of papers they had brought with them.

'This pile is what our Algiers Mission workers have sent us. There are stories, parables, lessons and much else besides,' Lilias said, putting the papers apart from the others.

'I'll lay your paintings over here,' Blanche suggested. 'There are quite a lot! And I'll pile your notes and ideas beside them.'

'Keep your writing apart from mine,' suggested Lilias. 'Or we'll get in a muddle.'

The pair tidied and piled, sorted and filed all the papers and paintings and notes of ideas they had brought with them.

'There's enough to keep us going for the whole three months and more,' concluded Blanche. 'And our Arab neighbours thought we were off on a long relaxing holiday.'

'Would you rather be doing that?' Lilias asked, knowing the answer already.

'No,' replied her friend. 'I want to get on with the Lord's work.'

The particular work the Lord had for them to do in Cairo was to write books for boys that would be sent out monthly to Arab lads who were usually very eager to read. Then there was writing to be done for women, especially the young women whom they had taught to read. And they hoped to write for girls too, booklets that would teach them about Jesus, while helping them to learn to read.

'Arab people just love beautiful colours,' Lilias said, as she worked on a painting of a plant with its roots digging deep into soil. 'The lovelier a book is, the more likely they are to buy it and read it.'

Over their months in Cairo the two women wrote in the mornings, and their afternoons were spent doing more writing or drawing or painting. The books were complicated to do because the hope was that they could be translated into different languages.

'How will this work?' someone asked.

Blanche explained. 'The Arabic ones are no problem. They are just printed as normal with the illustrations put where they fit in the text. Now imagine all the writing being taken away and only the illustrations left. That's what will happen with the others. Then the writing can be translated into other languages and put in the blank spaces.'

'I think I understand,' was the rather puzzled reply.

Blanche showed him some sheets with only the illustrations printed on them.

'The text will go in these spaces,' she said.

The man's face lit up. 'Now I understand,' he said. 'That's very clever.'

At the end of their three month 'holiday' the women packed to go back to Algiers.

'We'll come again next year for three months, if God lets us,' they told the printer, 'and get on with some more writing.'

That's exactly what happened.

Changes

During World War 1 missionaries were not able to get back to the U.K. for a summer break. Lilias's yearly timetable changed to be something like this. In the early part of the year she travelled round as many village mission stations as she could, working wherever she went rather than just visiting other missionaries. Spring brought the annual conference at Dar Naama. The summer months were spent at Blida and then it was back to Rue Du Croissant to do all the Algiers Mission Band's organising work – and what a lot of it there was!

In 1918, not long before the war ended, Lilias and Blanche were at Dar Naama to spend some weeks writing.

'It's not possible to write at Rue du Croissant,' Lilias decided. 'There's too much going on all the time. Even though the house is rambling, we can always be found.'

Blanche agreed. At Dar Naama there was the peace and quiet they needed. It was during their writing weeks that Blanche became ill and, after a week of being poorly, she died and went home to Jesus.

'It was thirty years ago today that we came to Algeria,' Lilias remembered. Then she bowed her head and thanked God for Blanche who had been such a dear and good friend.

Instead of going back to Rue du Croissant, Lilias stayed in Dar Naama and continued her work there.

'Lilias and Helen must miss Blanche so much,' said one of the other missionaries. 'They worked together for so long.'

'And they are not young themselves,' her friend commented.

'I know. Lilias is sixty-five now and Helen is nearly ten years older than her.'

'Not only that, neither of them has good health.'

Both women thought about Lilias's heart condition and wondered how long they would have the two original missionaries with them.

Over time Dar Naama became Lilias's home rather than Rue du Croissant in Algiers. The climate was cooler there and it was an easier place to live. Eventually it became the headquarters of the Algiers Mission Band.

'The work keeps on growing,' Lilias Trotter wrote to her brother. 'Since the war ended we have a number of new missionaries. And new missionaries allow us to start new work.'

She then went on to describe a new mission station being set up 300 miles south of Algiers.

'We seem to have reached the point where opportunities are opening on every side, and can be entered as fast as God sends men, women and money.'

She sat back and thought how different it was from the years when the government made things so difficult.

There was a new young missionary in the room with Lilias and she decided to tell her a little about the history of the Algiers Mission Band.

'In the early days we travelled by train to the main towns and finished our journeys to the villages however we could, often by camel. As the train chugged along we could see villages on the hillsides. We didn't know they were there because we saw houses, we knew because of the prickly pear bushes round about them. But we couldn't get to these villages because they were so far from train stations. I used to wonder if we'd ever reach them.'

The young woman was very interested.

'Now that we have motor buses going along the main roads missionaries can get off and stay for a few days in one village and then get on the bus to the next one.'

What Lilias had written to her brother was quite true, there were so many new opportunities.

It was springtime in 1921 when Lilias went back to the town of Tozeur. She first went there twenty-six years before that.

'Back then the name of Jesus had never been spoken in Tozeur and now we have two men, brothers brought up in the town, running the mission work there,' she said.

Lilias's travelling companion smiled. She had heard this story so often because it was one of her old friend's favourites. When they arrived, the young woman was a little surprised that the brothers lived in a real tumbledown house. But that was to change. Six weeks later, as they prepared to leave, Lilias had managed to arrange for it to be much more homely – not at all posh, she wouldn't have approved of that – just more comfortable.

'The brothers will work there all year round,' said Lilias, as they travelled back to Dar Naama. 'God is so good!'

When Lilias returned home she had a very different and interesting job to do.

'What are you thinking about?' Helen asked her. 'And why are you smiling like that?'

Her old friend explained that the brothers at Tozeur (they were called Ali and Amar, common Arab names) had asked her to find good Christian wives for them.

'I never found a husband for myself,' she joked. 'Now they want me to find wives for them.'

After much prayer and a great deal of thought the two men were married to the women that Lilias suggested. And they must have been very pleased with her choice because from then on she became known as something of a matchmaker!

'It is a beautiful thing to do,' Lilias told Helen. 'And it's really important that Christians only ever marry other Christians because that's what the Bible says is right.'

Beautiful Things

Two years later Lilias had an adventure. She had travelled many thousands of miles over Algeria on many different kinds of transport.

'Guess some of the ways I've travelled around your wonderful country,' she asked a group of children in El Oued. She was thrilled to be back there!

'Train!' yelled one little boy.

'Camel,' said another.

'I think you sometimes went by bus,' said an older girl. 'And I guess you've gone by donkey too.'

Lilias said that they were all right. Then she went on to tell them about the van that had been made for a lion tamer and his lion. The children sat with their mouths wide open.

'And today I am going on a new and exciting vehicle,' she said. 'Can you guess what it is?'

Because citrouens travelled regularly to El Oued the children were able to guess. And that day Lilias climbed on to her first citrouen. Later, back home in Dar Naama she told her friends about it.

'They are amazing!' she said, her eyes lighting up at the memory. 'Citrouens are like small tanks with caterpillar tracks and they go up and over desert sand

dunes easily. In fact, the journey from Touggourt to El
Oued took four days on a camel when I first went there
but it only takes ten hours on a citrouen.'

Some of the younger missionaries smiled at each
other at the thought of the elderly Lilias racing up and
down sand dunes on a small tank!

Lilias Trotter had to go on an even longer journey
when she went back to England in 1924. On her return
she was poorly and her friend Helen insisted on calling
out a doctor.

'You are exhausted and your heart is not good,'
she was told. 'You must stay in bed and have quiet
days now.'

The doctor probably meant Lilias to stay in bed and
do nothing, but that wasn't her style at all. She did stay
in bed because she was too weak to do anything else.
But I want you to imagine her bed. There were books
on it for her to read. To one side were sheets of paper
with names on them – names of people she wanted to
remember in her prayers. On the other side was a folder
of papers all about the work of the Algiers Mission
Band, plans to be made and work to be discussed. Then
there was her paint box and brushes on a little table
beside her and several sheets already painted.

'What is that?' Helen was asked, some months later.

'It's a book Lilias has written when she was meant
to be resting in bed.'

'What is it?'

Helen turned the pages slowly to let her friend see
the absolute beauty that she held in her hands.

'It's a book of paintings of Algeria,' she said. 'It's
called 'Between the Desert and the Sea.''

The two women sat down and paged through the book slowly.

'It is perfectly beautiful,' smiled Helen. 'And every brushstroke has been done with love.'

Now that Lilias Trotter was too weak to go and visit people, they came to see her. Even Ali and Amar and their families came all the way from Tozeur. After they went away she wrote about their visit in her journal.

'When someone is ill they crowd into the room and sit and look at the patient. Sometimes, if the patient is very ill, they start the death wail. They just don't understand that sometimes ill people need to be alone and quiet. Ali and Amar's wives just stood and looked kindly at me, then they hugged me and I could see tears in their eyes.'

'Then came Ali,' she wrote, 'who smiles joyfully over everything. Amar stood at the door, not quite sure what to do. He couldn't find words to say, but he gave me a lovely leather pouch decorated in Algerian embroidery and left.'

Lilias was very short of breath, probably because of her heart condition. For the rest of her life she often found it difficult to speak and only said a few words at a time. Despite that she wrote one last book as she sat propped up in her bed at Dar Naama. Lilias Trotter hadn't any thought of retiring!

Lilias was no longer able to be out of bed apart from those times she needed to be helped to the chair in order for her sheets to be changed. But all this didn't stop Lilias from praying. In fact, prayer became the work of the last months of her life. And she was thrilled when an Arab man she'd been praying for became a Christian.

As Lilias became weaker and weaker, God did a beautiful thing. Do you remember Francis and Reba Brading, the early Algiers missionaries who had to go home because the doctor said their children would not survive the heat? Well, by the time Lilias was in bed all the time, one of the Bradings' daughters was a missionary with the Algiers Mission Band. It was her job to nurse Lilias. Not only that, but her mother Reba went out to visit them. Lilias told her old friend Reba, 'Your little girl has crept into the cockles of my heart.'

And so it was that on 27th August 1928, surrounded by people she loved, Lilias Trotter lay in bed. Helen Freeman, who had gone to Algeria with her, was there and Lilias told her old friend that she could see many, many beautiful things. Lilias was about to leave earth and go to heaven. Nothing could be more beautiful than going there and seeing Jesus face to face.

By then the thirty missionaries serving God with the Algiers Mission Band were working in fifteen different parts of Algeria. Today the Band is part of Arab World Ministries, which still reaches out to Arab people in Algeria and many other countries too, telling them about the Lord Jesus.

Lilias Trotter
Timeline

1853	Isabella Lilias Trotter born in Marylebone, London to a wealthy family.
1853	Crimean War begins.
1865	Lilias's father dies.
1866	Alfred Nobel invents dynamite.
1876	Lilias travels to Italy with her mother and meets the famous artist John Ruskin who was impressed with her sketches.
1878	Lilias's mother dies.
1879	Thomas Edison demonstrates his new incandescent light bulb.
1884	Lilias becomes ill after undergoing surgery.
1887	Lilias applies as a candidate to the North African Mission, but is rejected due to her health.
1888	Lilias sails to Algiers independently with two other women: Blanche Haworth and Lucy Lewis.
1893	Lilias and Blanche travel to El Kantara.
1895	Lilias and Blanche travel to Tunisia. Lilias returns to England for six months to recover from exhaustion.
1900	Helen and Lilias travel to Tolga and rent a house.
1901	Lilias and Blanche settle into a local house in Tolga.

1902	Government officials and some local people make life difficult for Lilias and Blanche.
1903	Lilias starts to write parables in Arabic script and does drawings and paintings to illustrate them.
1905	Russian revolution.
1906	Work in Algeria improves and Algiers Mission Band is formed.
1907	Five new workers join the Algiers Mission Band.
1908	Copies of Luke's Gospel, printed in ordinary Arabic, arrive in Algeria.
1909	Twenty missionaries now working with Algiers Mission Band.
1911	Ten more missionaries join the Algiers Mission Band.
1914	World War I begins.
1915	Lilias and Blanche travel to Cairo for three months.
1918	Lilias and Blanche spend some weeks writing at Dar Naama. Blanche dies.
1921	Lilias returns to Tozeur.
1924	Lilias's health deteriorates.
1928	Lilias dies in Algiers, Algeria.

Thinking Further Topics

1. **London and some Londoners**

   Lilias was born into a wealthy family in London when Londoners thought that their city was the centre of the world. The Trotters were much better off than many people in London. Do you ever think about how much better off you are than many people in the world today? Are you grateful for what you have or sometimes do you just want more?

2. **Home and Away**

   Lilias had brothers and sisters. If there are other children in your family, how do you get on together? It's not always easy, but there are things we can do to help how we get on together. If you are an only child, how do you make and keep friends? Do you know that Jesus is the best of all friends?

3. **A New Home**

   Change is not always easy. Moving house is okay if you can still go to the same school and play with the same friends. Otherwise it can be very difficult. The best way to make friends is to be friendly. How can you be friendly among people you don't know? Until you make friends in a new place, try to remember that Jesus is with you, you are not alone.

4. **Holidays – Trotter Style**

   Being on holiday is great. But do you know where the word 'holiday' comes from? It's from 'holy day'. Long ago the only time people had off work were the church's holy days, special religious festivals. Nowadays we have regular holidays but they should be holy days too. Don't leave God behind when you go on holiday. Take your Bible with you and try to go to church when you are away from home.

5. **'You Don't Like Purple!'**

It's easy to let ourselves have likes and dislikes that are just plain silly. We say we don't like some foods just because they are not our favourites. And there are things we don't like doing because we like doing other things better. Try to remember that everything we have comes from God and to be grateful for what we are given. Imagine telling God, who created oranges, that we don't like what he made!

6. **A Big Decision**

Some decisions are easier than others. It is easier to choose between something we enjoy and something we don't enjoy. It's more difficult to choose between two good things. Lilias was doing a really good work in London and she was also a really good artist. But what did God want her to do? Lilias prayed for God to show her his will. Do you pray about decisions? In the Bible Jesus prayed before he chose his disciples.

7. **'A Ticket to Algiers, please.'**

Lilias and her two friends set out for Algeria to be missionaries there. If you are a Christian, God might call you to serve him overseas. But, even if he doesn't do that, God wants every Christian to be a missionary. Some are called to go to faraway countries and many more are called to be missionaries right where they are, in their own schools, in their own towns and sometimes in their own families.

8. **Finding Their Way Around**

When Lilias and her friends arrived in Algiers they didn't know anyone at all. One of the first places they went to was the church where they met others who knew and loved the Lord Jesus. It's good to make friends and better still to make Christian friends. You don't have to talk about church all the time! But you'll understand each other and encourage each other as you follow the Lord together.

9. **Like Playing Houses**

Lilias and her friends had never looked after themselves before they moved to Algeria. They had to learn to cook and clean, to shop and do other housekeeping things. That was a whole new experience for them. They weren't afraid to try new things in order to serve Jesus. And they didn't think that it was beneath them to do humble housework. God wants us to be humble rather than proud.

10. **Learning Arabic**

The three young missionaries had to learn Arabic. They found a good teacher and learned from him. It was very hard work. Do you work hard at your lessons? God has given us minds to think with and hands to do things with, and we have to learn to use our minds as much as we have to learn to use our hands. Studying hard at school is part of finding out what gifts God has given us.

11. **The Wordless Book**

Here is a challenge – use plain paper and crayons or felt pens to make your own little wordless book. When you have made it, put it beside your Bible and use it to remind you what the gospel is. Test yourself to see if you remember what the colours represent. The colours are black, red, white, green and gold.

12. New Arrivals

When new missionaries arrived to join Lilias and her friends, they were complete strangers to the city. They didn't know anyone and they had so much to learn. When someone new comes to live next door, or joins your class at school, how could you help to make them feel at home? Would you invite a new friend to church or Sunday school?

13. Home!

After searching for a long time the missionaries found a house that was just right. It was big enough for them all to live and work in, but it was also the kind of place where visitors would feel welcome. The Bible tells us to be hospitable. That means that we should make others welcome in our homes, our hearts and our friendships. How could you do that?

14. Desert Rain

Lilias was an artist and that helped her to really look at what was around her. God doesn't just want artists to do that. He made all the things we see around us: the trees, birds, plants, hills, clouds, flowers … everything. Having made them, God wants us to really enjoy them. Here's something to do. Every day take a really long hard look at something God has made and try to draw it from memory.

15. A Mirage?

Lilias told the children she met that she had good news for them. Do you know what is the best news in the world? Look up John 3 verse 16 in your Bible and you'll discover the best news in the world. When we hear good news we want to pass it on. Can you think of anyone to whom you could pass on the best news in the world?

16. Mahfoud, Dahman and Mohammed

These three older boys became Christians and they went to Lilias to ask how they could help the missionaries in their work. If you are a Christian, you'll want to find ways of helping others too. You could ask your Sunday school teacher or minister if there are any ways you could help in your church. Remember this wonderful fact – when you are helping others you are serving Jesus!

17. Lilias's Journal

Lilias kept a journal, a kind of big diary, and she wrote in it what she did, where she went, how she felt and what she was thinking. That helped her to remember things years later. It is because of her journals that we know so much about her even though she lived a long time ago. You might like to think about keeping a notebook of things that you've learned about the Lord and ways he has answered your prayers.

18. Children Everywhere!

There were so many children living round about the missionaries that they ran classes especially for them. Look up Matthew 19 verses 13-15 in your Bible to see who else was interested in spending time with children. Jesus, who is the Son of God, was also a really, truly boy. He knows and remembers what it is like to be a child and he understands. Do you know that you are precious to Jesus?

19. The Map-maker

Lilias was good at drawing maps as well as being good at drawing flowers and scenes and people. She drew maps of Algerian towns to help her plan their missionary work. Do you try to plan things or do you just go from one thing to another, according to what you feel like at the time? Planning helps us to get things done. For example, it is good to plan to read your Bible and pray every day rather than just doing it when you remember and are not too tired.

20. Hard Times

Being a missionary was not always easy and Lilias and her friends had some really hard times. Every Christian has hard times, even those your age. Perhaps you are being laughed at for going to church, or it may be that your parents don't understand, or your school wants you to do things on a Sunday. Jesus had hard times too and he understands. Pray about how to cope with hard times and ask him to help you through them.

21. Dar Naama

Being a Christian is not hard all of the time. In fact, sometimes it is very joyful. When we go home to heaven our lives will be joyful all the time for all the difficulties will have passed. Meanwhile we have to find ways to cope with the mixture of difficulty and joy that we meet day by day. That's where Christian friends come in for they understand us and we understand what they are going through too.

22. Digging for Water

Lilias was very serious about her work. Because she knew that people would not go to heaven when they died, if they didn't believe in Jesus, she was serious about telling them about him. Yet she was good fun too and enjoyed games and laughter. We mustn't think that God wants us to be serious all the time. Life is a mixture of all different feelings.

23. Growing Old

As Lilias grew older and less able, God still gave her work to do for him. There's no retirement for Christians as they want to serve Jesus as long as they live on earth. Can you think of some ways to serve Jesus as a young person? Now think about some of the elderly Christians you know and watch how they serve the Lord. Perhaps two ways they do that is by encouraging you and praying for you.

24. Changes

When Lilias was so poorly that she was in bed most of the time it was the job of a young missionary to look after her. Sometimes when they were together Lilias told her the history of the work in Algeria. History is really important because it is HIS-STORY – God's story. You will learn a great deal about the Lord by listening to old people telling you about what Jesus has done in the past.

25. Beautiful Things

Just before Lilias died she saw beautiful things and right after she died she saw Jesus. All Christians go to heaven when they die and all Christians will see Jesus. There can be no more beautiful experience than that. If you look up Revelation 21 verses 1-4 in your Bible, you'll discover a little bit about heaven. You'll discover some things that will not be in heaven – and it will be good to be rid of them!

About the Author

Irene Howat lives in Ayrshire, Scotland. She has written over fifty books, more than half of them for children. Irene also runs a children's on-line story-a-month club. Her life has been spent in various parts of Scotland, mainly in Argyll where her husband was a minister.

Having been brought up in the Land of Burns, Irene is interested in the Scots language and poetry and is both a prize-winning poet and a prize-winning author. Her other interests include reading, art and people. Relaxation usually involves pencils, paints, books, grandchildren or all of them together.

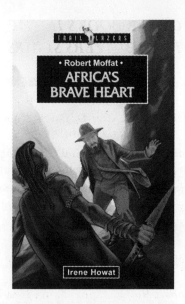

Robert Moffat: Africa's Brave Heart
by Irene Howat

Robert Moffat could think on his feet, and use his hands. He was strong, practical and just the sort of guy you needed to back you up when you were in difficulty. Not only that, he had courage – loads of it, and a longing to bring the good news of Jesus Christ to the people of Africa.

As Robert faced the dangers of drought, wild animals and even the daggers and spears of the people he had come to help, he used his unique collection of gifts and attributes to spread the gospel.

Africa's brave heart blazed a trail into the unknown, starting a work in that continent that continues today.

ISBN: 978-1-84550-715-2

OTHER BOOKS IN THE
TRAILBLAZERS SERIES

For a full list of Trailblazers, please see our
website: www.christianfocus.com
All Trailblazers are available as e-books

The Adventures Series
An ideal series to collect

Have you ever wanted to visit the rainforest? Have you ever longed to sail down the Amazon river? Would you just love to go on Safari in Africa? Well these books can help you imagine that you are actually there.

Pioneer missionaries retell their amazing adventures and encounters with animals and nature. In the Amazon you will discover tree frogs, piranha fish and electric eels. In the Rainforest you will be amazed at the armadillo and the toucan. In the blistering heat of the African Savannah you will come across lions and elephants and hyenas. And you will discover how God is at work in these amazing environments.

African Adventures by Dick Anderson
ISBN 978-1-85792-807-5

African Adventures by Dick Anderson
ISBN 978-1-85792-807-5
Amazon Adventures by Horace Banner
ISBN 978-1-85792-440-4
Antarctic Adventures by Bartha Hill
ISBN 978-1-78191-135-8
Cambodian Adventures by Donna Vann
ISBN 978-1-84550-474-8
Emerald Isle Adventures by Robert Plant
ISBN 978-1-78191-136-5
Great Barrier Reef Adventures by Jim Cromarty
ISBN 978-1-84550-068-9
Himalayan Adventures by Penny Reeve
ISBN 978-1-84550-080-1
Kiwi Adventures by Bartha Hill
ISBN 978-1-84550-282-9
New York City Adventures by Donna Vann
ISBN 978-1-84550-546-2
Outback Adventures by Jim Cromarty
ISBN 978-1-85792-974-4
Pacific Adventures by Jim Cromarty
ISBN 978-1-84550-475-5
Rainforest Adventures by Horace Banner
ISBN 978-1-85792-627-9
Rocky Mountain Adventures by Betty Swinford
ISBN 978-1-85792-962-1
Scottish Highland Adventures by Catherine Mackenzie
ISBN 978-1-84550-281-2
Wild West Adventures by Donna Vann
ISBN 978-1-84550-065-8

Start collecting this series now!

Ten Boys who used their Talents:
ISBN 978-1-84550-146-4
Paul Brand, Ghillean Prance, C.S.Lewis,
C.T. Studd, Wilfred Grenfell, J.S. Bach,
James Clerk Maxwell, Samuel Morse,
George Washington Carver, John Bunyan.

Ten Girls who used their Talents:
ISBN 978-1-84550-147-1
Helen Roseveare, Maureen McKenna,
Anne Lawson, Harriet Beecher Stowe,
Sarah Edwards, Selina Countess of Huntingdon,
Mildred Cable, Katie Ann MacKinnon,
Patricia St. John, Mary Verghese.

Ten Boys who Changed the World:
ISBN 978-1-85792-579-1
David Livingstone, Billy Graham, Brother Andrew,
John Newton, William Carey, George Müller,
Nicky Cruz, Eric Liddell, Luis Palau,
Adoniram Judson.

Ten Girls who Changed the World:
ISBN 978-1-85792-649-1
Corrie Ten Boom, Mary Slessor,
Joni Eareckson Tada, Isobel Kuhn,
Amy Carmichael, Elizabeth Fry, Evelyn Brand,
Gladys Aylward, Catherine Booth, Jackie Pullinger.

Ten Boys who Made a Difference:
ISBN 978-1-85792-775-7
Augustine of Hippo, Jan Hus, Martin Luther,
Ulrich Zwingli, William Tyndale, Hugh Latimer,
John Calvin, John Knox, Lord Shaftesbury,
Thomas Chalmers.

CHRISTIAN FOCUS PUBLICATIONS

Christian Focus / Christian Heritage / CF4K / Mentor

Christian Focus Publications publishes books for adults and children under its four main imprints: Christian Focus, CF4K, Mentor and Christian Heritage. Our books reflect our conviction that God's Word is reliable and Jesus is the way to know him, and live for ever with him.

Our children's publication list includes a Sunday School curriculum that covers pre-school to early teens, and puzzle and activity books. We also publish personal and family devotional titles, biographies and inspirational stories that children will love.

If you are looking for quality Bible teaching for children then we have an excellent range of Bible stories and age-specific theological books.

From pre-school board books to teenage apologetics, we have it covered!

Find us at our web page:
www.christianfocus.com

CF4•K
Because you're never
too young to know Jesus